A
Harlequin
Romance

WELCOME

TO THE WONDERFUL WORLD
OF *Harlequin Romances*

Interesting, informative and entertaining,
each Harlequin Romance portrays an appealing
and original love story. With a varied array
of settings, we may lure you on an African safari,
to a quaint Welsh village, or an exotic riviera
location — anywhere and everywhere that adventurous
men and women fall in love.

As publishers of Harlequin Romances, we're
extremely proud of our books. Since 1949,
Harlequin Enterprises has built its publishing
reputation on the solid base of quality and
originality. Our stories are the most popular
paperback romances sold in North America; every
month, eight new titles are released and sold at
nearly every book-selling store in Canada and the
United States.

A free catalogue listing all available Harlequin Romances
can be yours by writing to the

HARLEQUIN READER SERVICE,
(In the U.S.) M.P.O. Box 707, Niagara Falls, N.Y. 14302
(In Canada) Stratford, Ontario, Canada. N5A 6W4

or use order coupon at back of books.

We sincerely hope you enjoy reading
this Harlequin Romance.

Yours truly,

THE PUBLISHERS
   Harlequin Romances

MAN OF THE WILD

by

ROSEMARY CARTER

Harlequin Books

TORONTO • LONDON • NEW YORK • AMSTERDAM • SYDNEY • WINNIPEG

Original hardcover edition published in 1976
by Mills & Boon Limited

ISBN 0-373-01986-6

Harlequin edition published July 1976

Printed in Canada

CHAPTER ONE

'OH, how beautiful!' breathed Emma Anderson. She stopped the car, wound down the window, and stared into the bush. It was an idyllic scene, a scene out of a story-book.

In a grassy glade surrounded by ancient umbrella-shaped trees grazed a herd of buck – impala as she was soon to call them. With a flick of the ears they bent their graceful necks to the grass, quite unconcerned by her presence.

Only one animal, bigger than the others, and with horns – the father of the herd, Emma surmised – stood watching her. His strong body was poised and alert, his eyes bright and unwinking as he assessed her. Then, as if he was satisfied that she meant his herd no harm, he too went back to his grazing.

'I mustn't miss this,' thought Emma, picking up the camera that she had placed in readiness on the seat beside her. 'What a wonderful start to my trip!' As she busied herself with the light-meter she forced herself to be calm, yet every nerve was urging her to hurry and take the picture before the animals should take it into their heads to run away.

Finally she was ready. Leaning as far as she could out of the window, she turned the camera this way and that – but she was not satisfied. It all looked so different, so very disappointing, through the confining frame of the lens. She could see the big buck in the foreground, and one or two of the others who stood near him, but the babies, and the lovely trees in the background, these should be in the picture too. Emma knew what was wrong – it was the angle. If she could just move slightly nearer and over to the right . . . But that meant getting out of the car.

Momentarily there flashed through her mind the warning she had had at the gate. Oh, but she was being silly. The warning not to get out of the car surely did not apply in this case. For she could see there was no danger, and she was not going to venture far from the car. She opened the door and, taking her camera, moved to get the angle she needed.

So absorbed was she in what she was doing that she did not hear the car approach and stop. Not until the man was almost upon her did she become aware of him.

'Good gracious!' she burst out. 'You frightened me!'

'What the hell do you think you're doing?' He towered over her, his bushy eyebrows meeting in a scowl.

'Just taking a picture. The buck – they're so beautiful . . .'

'Couldn't you do that in the car?'

'Not properly. It was the angle, you see.'

'I don't, actually. Tell me, young lady, while we're on the subject of seeing – you didn't happen to see notices warning you not to get out of your car?'

'Yes, of course. But there's nothing here, except the buck, of course. In any case,' she continued, flushing under the disapproving gaze, 'you had no right to creep up on me like this. You frightened me.'

'Perhaps you think a lion might have been more considerate?' he drawled sarcastically.

'A lion?' she queried.

'There *are* lions in the Kruger National Park, madam.'

'I know that, but . . .'

'You don't think there's one for miles around.'

'Well, actually, I don't,' she flashed defiantly. 'I've driven quite far since I came into the Park, and these are the first animals I've seen.'

'There could be a lion behind that bush,' he said, and as she looked around, startled, he went on, 'There isn't – but there could be. And you wouldn't know till it pounced.'

'Oh, now, really,' she protested, forcing herself to be calm. 'It's so peaceful here.'

'Don't be deceived by all this tranquillity. This is Africa, not a zoo. There are plenty of wild beasts around that would just love a nip of what is, I'm sure' – he allowed himself a smile – 'sweet, soft meat.'

'I think you forget yourself,' she said coolly.

'No, I don't think I do. There's a hefty fine for what you've just been doing. Count yourself lucky to get off that. Now, back into your car, and don't get out again until you're in camp.'

The man, tall and bronzed-looking, got into his jeep and drove off. Emma waited a few minutes before starting her own car. She was reluctant to meet up with him again.

Her hands trembled as she put the camera back in its case. She was more shaken by the encounter than she cared to admit. The man had been unspeakably rude, or perhaps arrogant was the better word. What harm, after all, had she done? She had not ventured more than a few feet from her car. Had there been anything frightening she could have made a dash for safety in no time. Besides, the buck would not have been grazing so peacefully if there had been any danger. No, she decided, the man had just been nasty.

She drove slowly – the speed limit in the Park was twenty-five miles an hour – and as she drove she stared into the bush. She had driven some distance now, and was seeing animals with increasing frequency. Every now and then she stopped, once to smile at a warthog that scampered its clumsy way across the road, another time to

7

watch a giraffe, majestic and lofty, nibbling leaves from a tall tree. And often, more often than anything else, she saw impala, springing a graceful arch over the road in front of her, grazing in sun-dappled clearings, or just standing, motionless, bodies all turned in the same direction, sniffing the wind.

'I'm going to love this,' she thought with a sudden leaping of the heart. 'Three months of driving through this beautiful countryside. Hours spent at drinking places with the camera beside me. It won't seem like work at all.'

The sun was high in the sky and Emma was beginning to feel hungry when she rounded a bend and saw several cars standing quite still in the road. At first she thought there had been an accident, then she noticed people were all looking in the same direction. Some were peering through binoculars, others were pointing. All the cars, regardless of the direction in which they had been travelling, were parked on the same side of the road. Clearly, something was happening.

Puzzled, Emma drew alongside a small blue car and looked into the bush. A little further down the road a herd of impala grazed quietly, but at the spot on which the people in the cars seemed to have focused, she could see nothing at all.

'What is it?' Leaning out of the window, she managed to attract the attention of a woman in the blue car. 'What is everybody looking at?'

'Lions.' The woman gestured to a clump of trees.

'Lions?'

'Three. There behind the trees.'

'But I can't see a thing,' said Emma.

'I know. They're lying down.'

Emma put her binoculars to her eyes and swept the bush. 'I can't see them,' she called.

8

'They're there. Caught a glimpse of a mane just now.'

'You did?'

'I think so anyway. With all the underbrush and the anthills you can never be sure. Still, it would be nice to tell the folks back home that I'd seen a lion.'

'Mm.' Doubtfully Emma peered through the thick bush. 'However did you manage to spot them in the first place?'

'We didn't. The people in that car over there – the red one – they were the lucky ones. The lions crossed the road in front of them on their way back from the river.' The woman sighed. 'They could lie there for ages, I suppose.'

'Well, I don't intend waiting for them to get up. I want to get to camp.' Carefully Emma began to edge her car around the motionless vehicles. In a sombre mood she drove on. Three lions lying behind a bush – and to look at the peaceful countryside it was hard to believe anything more dangerous than a butterfly stirred anywhere near.

Without exceeding the speed limit she drove steadily and with no further stops, for all at once she had become eager to reach the camp. The next three months would give her plenty of time to drive around and look for animals. Right now what she wanted most was to settle down and unpack, have a bath and something to eat.

And so at last she came to Skukuza. Just inside the gate she stopped the car, letting the sensations of colour and bustle and activity wash over her.

As she was about to drive on, her attention was caught by a grey muddy scuffling nearby. Scarcely able to believe her eyes, Emma got out of the car and went nearer. Warthogs! In camp! Impossible – and yet there they were, rolling over and over in the squelchy mud near the dripping tap. Nobody was in sight. Perhaps nobody knew they were there. She must find someone in charge and report this, before anyone could get hurt.

'Oh, those warthogs,' laughed the woman in the office a few minutes later. 'Funny little things, aren't they? They love that mudhole by the tap.'

'So then you know they're here?' Emma asked, feeling a little foolish.

'Yes. That little family has adopted us. They're used to people now, and don't do any harm.' She rummaged through a pile of papers. 'Now, let's see. Ah, here we are – Miss Emma Anderson. And you're staying three months?'

'Yes.'

'Lovely. You'll be almost one of us, in that case. The lads will be glad to have a new female face around.'

'The lads?' Emma asked curiously.

'Game rangers, personnel about the camp. Now, Miss Anderson, I have a nice little hut for you. Stroke of luck, really, that it happened to be available. I'll just find someone to take you there, and . . . Oh, here's Lance Mason.' She paused as a young man came nearer. 'Lance, you're going off duty? Oh, good. This is Miss Emma Anderson, the lass who plans to stay with us a few months. Would you mind showing her to her hut?'

'I'd be delighted to.' He smiled at Emma, showing even white teeth in a pleasantly tanned face. 'Where did you leave your car? Over in the car-park? Let's go, then.'

Half an hour later Emma sat on the broad verandah outside the restaurant, looking out over the river. Lance Mason had taken her to her hut, telling her he would be back a little while later when he would treat her to some lunch. She had just finished unpacking when he had knocked at her door, and they had walked to the restaurant together.

Now, as she ate a fruit salad with ice-cream, she felt

happy and at ease. The holiday atmosphere of the camp was exhilarating. The big verandah was filled with people relaxing over their cool drinks and swapping stories of what they had seen that morning. Through the air wafted the smell of charcoal fires, and at the fence looking over the river, people stood with field-glasses, gazing beyond the river into the endless bush.

'Not an animal to be seen,' said Emma, her eyes sweeping the panoramic vista before her.

'You think so?' Lance laughed. 'Look there ... no, there, where my finger's pointing. Can't you see it?'

'I ... no ... where?'

'Further to the right. Yes, by that clump of trees. Do you see a bit of brown?'

'But there's brown all over,' Emma pointed out.

'Ah, but there's brown and brown. What I'm looking at is a giraffe. Yes, you see it now. It's moving towards the river.'

'Is it coming here?' Emma asked excitedly.

'Very likely. Could take ages, though. It may be in no hurry. But if you waited long enough you'd probably see it.'

'In that case ...' She turned to him. 'I suppose there must be lots of game ...'

'You've just got to be lucky,' he explained.

'I hope I will be. That's why I'm here.'

'I was going to ask you about that,' Lance said curiously. 'I wondered what a girl from England – oh, yes, I recognize that accent and the peaches and cream complexion – proposes to do in the Park for three months.'

Her eyes left his and rested on the activity all around her. 'A friend is writing a book,' she said presently. 'He's asked me to do the photography.'

'Do you know a lot about animals, then?'

'Very little.'

'Then why ... I'm sorry, I didn't mean to be rude...'

'I don't know a lot about animals,' said Emma, 'but I do know quite a bit about photography. I was given the opportunity and I thought I'd like to do it.'

She fell silent, thinking of Jimmy to whom she would have been married by now if ... if ... But there, it had happened, and she did not intend telling Lance about it. It was enough that this opportunity to get away for a while had presented itself.

'Do you think I'll manage?' was all she said.

'I'm sure of it. I'll take you out whenever I have a chance. Show you the ropes, so to speak.'

'How kind of you. Are you a game ranger?'

'No. I do some work in the shop and the office.' He grinned. 'Man of many parts!'

'I see.' She smiled back at him. 'Mr. Mason...'

'Lance, please.'

'And I'm Emma. Lance, I was wondering about the warthogs – I saw them when I arrived here. I thought animals never get into the camps.'

'As a rule they don't. That little family is somewhat of an exception. Skukuza wouldn't be the same without its warthogs. Still, if you intend going to some of the smaller camps it's a good idea not to wander around outside very late at night, when the lights and the fires are out.'

'You mean...'

'The odd hyena sometimes gets over the fence in search of scraps.' He laughed at the concern in her face. 'Don't look so alarmed. Nobody ever comes to harm in the Park.'

'If they keep to the rules.' Emma and Lance looked up at the man who stood beside their table.

'You!' Emma found herself flushing as she looked into the hard tanned face of the man she had met a few hours earlier.

'Stewart? Emma?' Lance was puzzled as he glanced from one to the other. 'You know each other?'

'We've – met.' The grey eyes in the tanned face challenged her. 'Though I can't say we've had a formal introduction.'

When Lance had introduced them he said, 'I don't understand. What was that remark about keeping to the rules?'

'I happened to be passing your table and couldn't help overhearing the conversation.' Stewart glanced wickedly at Emma. 'The remark just seemed appropriate. There *are* animals in the Park, you know, Miss Anderson. I believe some lions made a kill not far from here this morning.'

'You are really the most impossible ...' Emma burst out, stopping when she found she was talking to a fast retreating figure. 'Is he always so rude?' she asked after a moment, watching the tall athletic man stride away.

'Not exactly the most diplomatic of men, our Stewart Bristow,' Lance observed, watching her curiously.

'Does he work here?'

'He's a game ranger.'

'Oh!' So she would have to face him often.

'I didn't realize you two had met,' Lance was saying.

'Not a social meeting. Actually, it was quite ridiculous. You see ...' Emma found herself relating what had happened. 'Was it really so dangerous? I only stood at the side of the car.'

'Let's say it wasn't very wise, Emma. In fact, you were probably lucky to get away without a fine.' He smiled at her reassuringly. 'Cheer up. After all, nothing happened, and next time you'll know better. I have the afternoon off today. How about coming for a drive with me? We might just be lucky and spot something for the camera.'

Emma sat forward in her seat, her eyes bright with

excitement, as the car moved out of the camp gates. At a stone beacon showing the names of camps and the roads leading to them Lance turned left.

'Ever heard of the Lower Sabie Road?' he asked her.

'The Lower Sabie Road?' she exclaimed. 'Oh, yes, I've read about it. Isn't it one of the great game park roads of the world?'

'That's right.'

'And we'll be driving down it?'

'You're on it now, my dear.' He took his hand from the wheel and squeezed hers briefly. 'I hope we'll see enough game to make your first day in the Park a memorable one.'

'This is marvellous!' Emma glued her eyes to the slowly passing landscape. 'I can't believe I'm really here. Oh, Lance, this *is* exciting!'

'Don't expect to see animals all the time,' he said gently. 'This is not a zoo, you know, with animals lined up by the roadside.'

'Not a zoo.' It was the second time that day she had heard these words. The first time had been that morning, only then they had been spoken angrily. Contemptuous eyes in a tanned gaunt face. She shook her head impatiently. Stewart Bristow was not going to spoil her enjoyment of this day, and all the other other days to come. 'I know it's not a zoo,' she said lightly. 'We're going awfully slowly, aren't we, Lance? I mean, I know the speed limit is twenty-five miles an hour, but aren't we doing far less?'

'If you kept to the speed limit you'd be going too fast,' Lance told her. 'You want to see animals, and for that you *must* go slowly. Otherwise, unless they're just basking by the roadside you'd never see them.'

'Of course. Oh, Lance, oh, look!' Baboons and monkeys, swinging from the branches of trees. Running

14

through the grass, sitting on the road in front of the car.

'Close your window,' Lance ordered.

'Oh, but . . .' She had been leaning out of the car and turned back to him.

'Close it!' he snapped. 'Quickly!'

A little bewildered, she complied, just as an animal, bigger than the others, came out of the bush.

'A male baboon,' Lance told her.

'And . . . the window?'

'Dangerous. Dangerous as can be.'

The massive beast padded towards the car, and hoisted itself up, its forelegs on Emma's window, the ugly face inches away from her own.

'Heavens!' She drew back in alarm.

'Unprepossessing brute, isn't he? Oh, no, Emma,' Lance laughed, 'don't be frightened. He can't get to you now the window's closed.'

'What would happen if it were open?'

'He'd probably scalp you,' Lance said seriously. 'He'd seize your hair in those strong fists of his and there's little you could do to make him let go.'

'I hadn't realized' – she was trembling – 'I hadn't realized it was so dangerous.'

'It's not,' he said cheerfully. 'When people keep to the rules they come to no harm – Stewart's right about that. Animals don't attack people in cars. But they *are* wild.'

'Yes. Yes, I know . . .'

'It's something many people seem to forget. You've no idea how many people get out of cars, or watch animals with their windows down. They seem to think they're just like circus beasts – tame, and put on show for the tourists. Why, one man wanted an elephant to charge so he could film it and show it to the folks back home. Know what he did? He pelted the elephants with oranges.'

'Good gracious! Did he get his picture?'

'He was lucky he got away with his life. There's nothing sillier than trying to play games with an elephant. But then it's amazing how silly people can be.'

'Like me,' she said ruefully.

'You've not been all that bad,' he said gently, and smiled at her. 'Put it down to experience and don't do it again.'

If only Stewart Bristow had it in him to be so understanding, Emma thought. If only ... Then she thrust the thought of him determinedly from her mind. She was not going to think again about that obnoxious man.

Two more cars had stopped to watch the monkeys and baboons. A child had turned its window down very slightly – not far enough for a monkey to get in, Emma observed – and was throwing crisps on to the ground. The big baboon padded contemptuously away. The babies scrambled and fought over the food.

A monkey jumped on to the bonnet of the car. An empty crisp packet was pushed through the open slit and the animal grabbed it and pushed it vigorously into its mouth. Emma could not help laughing. 'How will they get the monkey off?' she asked.

'It will jump,' said Lance. 'The monkeys on the Lower Sabie Road are used to cars and people. I suppose they associate people with food. They love to jump on to cars and, of course, the people adore them – especially the children.'

'I can see I will too.' Emma was still laughing as they drove on.

They drove slowly and in silence, Emma watching the bush on her side, Lance on his. For a while they saw almost nothing, but Emma relaxed, enjoying the scenery.

The road followed the course of the river. On one side the vegetation was very much like that which she had seen during the morning – thorny bushes and the umbrella-shaped acacias. On the other side of the road, the river side, there were tall reeds, and the trees were greener, denser, more lush.

Now and then, when the road wound closer to the river, she would see the water glinting through a break in the trees, calm and wide and very green. Then the road would curve away from it again, but always the reeds were there, and the lushness.

They came to a part where Emma looked about her in wonder and dismay. It was as if she were at a scene of some dreadful devastation, a place where a disaster had taken place. The trees were dead and dying, branches snapped and white, the grass trampled and dead. 'What's happened?' She turned to Lance. 'The lovely trees . . .'

'Elephants,' he told her.

'But – the trees . . .'

'Elephants eat leaves. Strange when you consider their bulk that they don't eat meat, but there it is. They rip the branches from the trees with their trunks. That's what all the havoc is about.' He glanced out of the window. 'Been along here quite recently.'

'How do you know?' she asked curiously.

'See those?' He gestured to the big black-ringed piles in the middle of the road. 'Elephant dung . . . and it's still steaming.'

'Will we see them?' she asked.

'If we're lucky.' Lance drove even more slowly now, his eyes moving constantly from the road to the bush.

They had driven a little further when they rounded a bend and came upon three cars parked in the road. At first glance it seemed as if there was nothing to see, but as they drew alongside a man leaned out of a car, pointed into the bush, and called, 'Three elephants in there.'

'I don't believe it,' Emma said, mystified.

'See that tree?' Lance was peering out of his window. 'The one behind the broken acacia. 'Can't you see something moving?'

'Yes.'

'There's an elephant through there. More than one elephant.'

'But it seems impossible!' Emma exclaimed, trying to visualize an elephant's great size.

'You might be surprised. The bush is very deceptive.'

'Lance, is it really worth waiting?' She was remembering the lions earlier that morning.

'I think so. They may be going down to the river soon.'

They had been waiting some time, and several more cars had drawn alongside, when all at once there was a flurry of movement from the bushes.

'Is that ... Why, it's an ear!' Emma exclaimed as she saw something flat and grey flapping above the greenery. 'It's ... Oh, Lance! It really *is* an elephant.'

The bushes parted as the elephant lumbered slowly through them and made for the road.

'He's tremendous!' breathed Emma. 'Just look at the size of his ears, and the trunk. Oh, Lance!' And then another elephant came through the bushes, and another, and then all three were swaying towards the road, stopping every now and then to curl a trunk around the branch of a tree.

'Look, Emma,' Lance said quietly.

'But I'm dreaming! It can't be!' Through the bushes came another elephant and then another. Elephants without number, it seemed to Emma.

She reached for her camera and was ready for them as they began to cross the road just in front of the car.

There must have been at least fifty of the great lumbering beasts – elephants of all sizes. Mothers and fathers and children and babies, all together in an orderly group as they padded across the road between the stationary cars. It was one of the most awe-inspiring sights Emma had ever seen.

And then they were out of sight. Minutes later she could hear them trumpeting as they crashed through the undergrowth to the river.

'Look, Emma, there they are.' Lance pointed through the trees.

'I know they're all down there, and yet I can see only three – oh, no, there's a fourth. Oh, look, that elephant's taken a trunk-full of water and now he's sprayed it back over himself.'

'That's the way an elephant baths,' said Lance.

The noise continued, the trumpeting and the splashing and the crashing of trees and branches. And then, perhaps twenty minutes later, Lance said, 'Camera ready? They're coming back again.'

And there they were. The whole troupe once more, padding across the road through the waiting cars. Into the bushes they went, mothers, fathers and the many children. Minutes later they had vanished completely from sight.

'Show's over.' Lance put the car into gear as the other vehicles began to move away. They were driving off when a small car came towards them, and without stopping drove over the very spot where only minutes earlier fifty elephants had crossed the road.

'Isn't it incredible?' Emma said wonderingly. 'Those people don't even know there are elephants just a little way from here.'

'That's the way it is in the Park,' Lance answered. 'It's just a matter of luck.

'It's going to be fun having you here,' he said when

they were nearly back at the camp. 'It gets lonely.'

'It does?' She looked at him curiously, thinking that Lance was so pleasant and outgoing that he must find it easy to make friends. 'The camp seems to bustle with people.'

'Mostly visitors. They stay a night or two and then move on. There's just about no social contact with them at all.'

'But there are people who live in the camp, aren't there?'

'Of course. Especially at Skukuza, as it's the biggest camp. There are always people about, working in the office, the library, the restaurant. But it's like a tiny village. We all know each other. It will be nice to have someone new – especially someone as super as you.' He looked at her and smiled.

'Thank you, kind sir,' she dimpled back at him. Then she ventured, 'There are the game rangers too, aren't there?'

Lance's face seemed to darken. Then he said, 'Thinking of Stewart?'

'Oh . . . oh, no. It was just a question.'

'Just a question. Of course. There *are* the game rangers.' He lapsed into silence as if he was considering whether to go further. Presently he said, 'Emma, advice from a pal. Be careful of Stewart.'

'Good heavens! What on earth are you telling me that for?'

'You find him attractive, don't you?'

'I hardly know the man,' Emma burst out. 'I've seen him exactly twice, a few minutes each time, and each time he was quite impossibly rude.'

'All right, perhaps I shouldn't have raised the subject.' He looked at her sombrely. 'But in case I'm right . . . Don't fall for him, Emma. You're a nice girl. I wouldn't like to see you break your heart over him.'

The afternoon shadows were deepening as they approached Skukuza. Once they stopped to watch a family of monkeys squabbling and jumping in the branches of a tree. Then Lance glanced at his watch. 'Time to get moving. Daren't get back to camp late in the evenings.'

They were driving through the big camp gates when he turned to her and said, 'Like to have a braai – a barbecue – with me? It's the typical camp way of eating, roasting meat over a charcoal fire.'

'I'd love that.' She was glad to see that his mood had lightened once more.

'Fine.' He opened the door of the car for her. 'I'll see you a little later, then.'

Emma stood by the fence looking over the river. The sun was setting and the bush, at this time of the day, had an indefinable air of mystery.

All about her in the camp she could hear the sounds of people getting ready for the evening meal. Somehow, the atmosphere of the camp seemed to have changed.

A little while ago she had wandered through the camp shop, walking with enjoyment but with no definite purpose from counter to counter, looking at the food counters, at the counters that held curios and stuffed monkeys, skin handbags and indigenous jewellery.

Most of all she enjoyed watching the people. The shop was a hub of gay activity as the holidaymakers thronged its passages, buying food for their supper. Men and women and children, relaxed and happy, moved through the shop carrying packets of frozen meat, lamb chops and steak and the sausage which she was to learn was called *boerewors*, the *boerewors* that was the standby of every barbecue or braai.

Trolleys were piled high with milk and fruit. Children

21

squabbled near the sweet counter. Fathers exchanged tall stories of the many lions they had seen that day, while mothers calculated how much food they needed, and looked round for children who seemed to have disappeared.

What fun it all was! Emma would have liked to join in the buying spree, but Lance had promised to treat her to a braai, and would be calling for her later at her hut.

She had left the shop after a while and wandered about the camp. Outside the bungalows coal fires were beginning to burn, and already the smell of charcoal and cooking meat wafted tantalizingly through the air.

Presently Emma walked down to the fence by the river. There was something about the broad stretch of water and the endless vista of bush beyond that fascinated her. She tried to imagine the hundreds of unseen animals, in those endless miles of thorn trees on the other side of the river, living and dying and bearing their young. She felt she could never get tired of this view. Three months here would pass all too quickly.

'See anything?' She had not heard him approach.

'No.' She glanced up, smiling instinctively, and found she was looking into the face of Stewart, the game ranger. Her smile froze.

'I won't bite.' He was grinning down at her. 'You're being very law-abiding right now.'

'I . . .' She bit back the words. It really would be childish to start another argument.

'Like it?' He stood beside her at the fence, leaning forward on his arms.

'Oh, yes. It's . . . it's fascinating,' she said a little breathlessly.

'The bush or the animals?' She looked up at him, quickly, but he was smiling.

'I meant the bush. I can't see any animals. It's too dark.

Though I don't doubt there's a lion behind every tree.' He laughed, and suddenly the tension between them was broken. 'No, it's the bush,' she continued. 'There's something about it. I can't seem to put my finger on it . . . can't give it a name. But there's a feeling of timelessness. As if . . . as if it stretched far away, for miles and miles without end, just like this.'

'Of infinity?' he said simply.

'Oh, yes, that's just what I meant. I couldn't think of the word to express it. But it's . . . well, I've never experienced anything quite like this before. In England . . .'

'I imagine you don't have this kind of landscape.'

'England is pretty. It's gentle and kind and very appealing. This . . .' For a moment she paused, searching for words to describe the intensity of feeling that the bush had stirred up in her. 'It's wild and rough and strong. There's nothing gentle about it, but it's beautiful, very beautiful. And so big.'

'Yes, it's big and wild,' he murmured.

'There's this feeling of tremendous space. Of horizons that are a thousand miles away.'

'And knowing that when you reach them the view will be the same again.'

'You know how I feel, don't you?' she asked curiously.

'Yes, Emma.' He had used her name for the first time, quite unselfconsciously. 'I know how you feel, because it's the way I feel. It's the reason I live here.'

She glanced up at him curiously. 'You've never wanted a different kind of life?'

'This type of country – living with animals, this is what I love.'

They were silent for a while as the darkness crept up on all sides of them. Then he touched her arm briefly and said, 'A peace-offering. Will you have supper with me?'

'Oh, Stewart, I can't.' Suddenly she knew she would

have given anything to eat with him now, and not to have to go back to her hut where Lance would be waiting for her.

'Booked up already?'

'I . . . I promised Lance I'd eat with him. He said something about a barbecue.'

'A braai. Better get the lingo right. All right, then,' he said lightly, and she knew the lovely atmosphere between them was shattered. 'You'd better get back, hadn't you?'

'Couldn't you join us?' she said quickly. 'Why can't we all . . .'

'Have a braai together? Lance and you and me? No, Emma, that wouldn't be Lance's style at all.'

'But . . .'

'Come.' He did not let her continue with what she was about to say. 'It's late. You must be hungry.'

'Will I see you again?' she blurted out, feeling foolish as soon as she had said it.

'Why, of course,' he answered, and she thought his tone was mocking. 'Skukuza's like a village, you know. You'll be seeing me around.'

The lovely mood that had pervaded her was broken. She stood by the fence a few moments longer, watching unhappily as the tall lean figure strode briskly away and was soon lost in the darkness. Did he think she was some cheap little flirt? The way he'd said, 'Booked up already?' Did he think she was just out to catch a man?

Angrily she shook her head. Was this why she had left England? Complications, men, marriage. The love affair with Jimmy that had turned so unhappy when he had decided to marry the boss's daughter just four weeks before their own marriage was to have taken place. Now she wondered whether she had ever really loved Jimmy, whether it had not been the idea of marriage to a handsome man she had been in love with. Be that as it may, the unhappiness, the humiliation and the recriminations, had all been real enough. It had been an absolute godsend when the offer to go to South Africa had turned up.

And now, when at last her mental well-being was nearly restored, she was certainly not going to have it destroyed again. Romance was just not on the agenda. The men she met would be acquaintances, even friends, but no more than that. She defied Stewart or Lance or any other man to destroy the peace of mind she had so painfully acquired.

'At last!' Lance was busy over a charcoal fire when she came to her hut.

'I'm sorry.' She was contrite. 'I didn't think you'd be here already.'

'That's okay. Though it did occur to me to wonder whether I'd been jilted.'

'Jilted?' The word shot from her lips.

'You know,' he looked up and his smile was whimsical, 'for Stewart.'

'For heaven's sake!' she burst out, really angry now. 'What on earth is that supposed to mean?'

'Relax, Emma. It's just a joke.'

'Oh!'

'Though you were so late in coming that I thought perhaps you'd decided to eat with Stewart instead.'

'No, I hadn't decided to eat with Stewart instead.' After a moment she added in measured tones, 'Though he *did* ask me.'

'He did?'

'Yes, Lance, he did. But let's get one thing straight between us. I owe nothing to any man, and that's the way I intend to keep it. I will be friends with whomever I please, whenever I please.'

'Whew!' Lance whistled as he took a step backwards.

'And what was that all about? A Women's Lib speech to a poor worthless male?'

'No. Just a declaration of independence.' She laughed a little shakily, forcing herself to relax. 'I lost my temper just now. Not over you – though you've unfairly had to bear the brunt of it. I'm sorry, Lance. Can . . . can we still be friends?'

'Of course.'

'And I'm forgiven?'

'It would be hard, sweet Emma, not to forgive you. Ever.'

'Oh, Lance, thank you.' She really was sorry now. 'Though I meant what I said.'

'Point taken. Now, here's the meat. A couple of lamb chops each and some *boerewors*.'

'Mm, they look delicious. How do I cook them?'

'You don't. I'll hold them over the fire,' Lance told her. 'A South African custom. At a *braaivleis* the men do the braaiing of the meat.'

'And the women?'

'They sit back and wait for it.' He laughed. 'The fire's ready. Would you like to prick the wors all over with a fork – that's it – and now, we'll sprinkle a little lemon juice over the meat. Ah, yes, and a dash of salt and pepper . . .'

'You're making my mouth water!' she smiled.

'That's the idea.' Lance produced an iron grid bent in two, with a long handle, and into it he neatly folded the meat. Then he laid it over the fire which by now was only softly glowing. Alongside the grid he placed four white beaded objects which Emma had never seen before.

'What are those?' she asked.

'Mealies.' Seeing her puzzled face, he chuckled and explained, 'Maize. Corn on the cob.'

'Lance, we'll never eat all this food.'

'We'll certainly give it a try.'

The smell of frying meat wafted through the air and suddenly Emma realized how hungry she was. Apart from the fruit salad and ice-cream at lunch-time she had had nothing all day.

'Mm, this is gorgeous. Absolutely scrumptious!' Hungrily she bit into the meat that Lance put on to her plate. 'Oh, Lance, this meat! I don't know when I enjoyed food so much. Why do people ever eat indoors and cook over stoves? Oops!' She quickly licked her fingers as the melting butter with which the mealies were drenched began to drip. 'These mealies are marvellous. Oh, yes, please, I'd adore another one.'

A *braaivleis* had a charm all its own, Emma discovered, so many qualities blending together to give it a special atmosphere. The charcoal smell and the crackling and hissing of the fire, the laughter that carried from neighbouring fires, overhead the vast African sky with its myriad stars, and all about the pervading sounds of the bush at night.

When they had finished their meal they went for a walk around the camp and Emma was enthralled with all she saw. Slowly they strolled past bungalows where children played in gowns and pyjamas while their parents washed up together, or sat chatting companionably over mugs of beer. They walked along the wall of the camp, past the gates where fires blazed.

They were walking through that part of the camp where the personnel had their quarters when Lance took her hand in his. Moments later, before she could react to the gesture, a tall lean figure strode their way. Emma had a momentary impulse to draw her hand away. Then she remembered the resolve she had made earlier that evening, and keeping her hand in Lance's she looked as directly as she was able into Stewart's face. 'Nice evening,' was all he said, impersonally, as he passed them without stopping.

Why had Lance chosen that particular moment to take her hand? Emma wondered. And then she thrust the thought from her. Lance had given her a delightful evening, displaying none of the rudeness and ill temper Stewart was capable of. If, feeling relaxed and replete, he had chosen to hold her hand while they walked it was nothing more than a gesture of friendship. Casting a quick look at his face and seeing the equable expression there, she knew she had been uncharitable. There was really no reason why he should have tried to provoke her – or Stewart.

'He ... he's so self-sufficient,' she observed a few moments later, taking it for granted that Lance would know what she meant.

'That he is.' Lance chuckled softly in the darkness. 'Now remember what I said and don't go breaking your heart over him. Shall we turn here and go down to the river?'

At the fence they leaned forward and stared into the blackness of the bush. Lance took out his cigarettes, offered her one, and when she refused, lit a cigarette for himself. It was dark by the river, with only the tiny red tip of the cigarette glowing in the darkness, and though they stood together they did not speak. Emma breathed deeply of the fragrant night air, absorbing the atmosphere around her.

All about them was a high shrill noise, a million crickets rubbing their legs together in a timeless song. 'The sound of Africa at night,' said Lance. Every now and then other sounds intruded themselves upon that endless shrilling. The laugh of a hyena, a small scuffling somewhere very near them in the long grass just beyond the fence, a bark like a dog's, which Lance said was the sound of a baboon. Once a low roar reverberated through the night and Emma jumped.

'That was a lion,' Lance said. 'Quite a sound when you're not used to it, isn't it?'

After a while it began to get chilly and Lance walked her back to her little hut. 'Sleep well.' He bent forward and, before she realized what he intended, he had dropped a fleeting kiss upon her hair. Then he was gone.

Sleep came slowly that night. For a long while Emma lay still, absorbing the sounds beyond her window. The camp had grown quiet, only the laughter of the attendants who looked after the fire still ringing in the darkness.

Once she heard a lion roar and wondered whether it was the same lion she had heard by the river. A lonely trumpeting came from somewhere far away, then all was still again.

'I'm going to love this,' Emma thought. 'There's something primitive and basic and earthy and marvellous about it all.' England and Jimmy seemed very far away. For the first time she realized that she had hardly thought about Jimmy that day, and when she had it was not with anguish. The healing was nearly complete.

So many things she had seen that day. She thought fleetingly of the two men she had met, and in the moments before sleep finally came to her an image swam before her eyes. Not Jimmy's image, but a sardonic face with mocking grey eyes and a crooked smile. And then that too dissolved as Emma slept.

CHAPTER TWO

EMMA had soon settled comfortably into the life of the camp. Very early, before the sun was up, she would open the door of her hut and stare out into the darkness that was just beginning to lift, before going back inside to dress. It was bitterly cold at this time of the morning, and she would wrap up warmly in jerseys and a jacket that could be discarded when the sun came out and it grew hot – and it could be very hot indeed during the day, she had discovered.

When she was dressed she would go to one of the enormous urns that bubbled all day with boiling water. Taking a cup and a little instant coffee, she would stir the boiling water into the cup.

This was a time she enjoyed. Cupping her cold hands around the hot cup, she would sip her coffee slowly as she ate a biscuit and watched the camp wake to the day.

All about her in the lifting darkness children in scarves and jerseys spilled excitedly out of their bungalows. Mothers filled thermos flasks with boiling water, while fathers wiped the dew from their windscreens.

In the Kruger National Park the camp gates open at dawn and close when the sun sets. No cars are allowed on the roads at night, for, as Lance had explained to her, the risks of running over animals on the unlit roads are high.

Emma had seen the clock at the gates, showing the opening and closing times for the day, and long before the camp opened in the morning, a long line of cars had already queued up in front of the gates. It seemed to her that many people were prepared to make the sacrifice of rising early, believing that it was at this time of the day, when the animals were returning from the rivers and water-holes after their morning drink, that there was the most chance of seeing game.

She loved the air of excitement that pervaded the camp at sunrise. It was a tingling atmosphere, pulsating and gay. At sunset people might be weary and hot after a long day on the road, but in the early morning they were eager to get going, filled with the ever-present hope that on this day they would see lions.

Even in her short stay in the Park Emma had become infected with the obsession for the big cats. It was rare to drive for hours without seeing any animals at all. One could almost take it for granted that one would see impala and monkeys, even giraffe, and, if one was lucky, elephants. But it was the big cats, the lions and leopards and cheetahs, that were like the hunters' cherished scalps. There was an indefinable aura about the king of beasts that seemed to make it more exciting to crane one's head over the tops of stationary cars in order to see the royal tail of a lion disappearing into the bush than to sit in comfort and watch a family of monkeys at play.

'You see, lady,' a man, one of the visitors to Skukuza, told her as they queued together to pay for their purchases in the camp shop. 'Now, when I get back home I can tell the folks I saw a lion. It doesn't matter that I only saw its head, because the lazy lovely brute wouldn't get on to his feet. Fact is, I saw it. I saw it with my own two eyes.'

Emma would join the queue at the entrance to the camp, waiting for the gates to open, when the cars, like a long caravan, moved slowly on to the roads.

The early morning was exhilarating. Bushes sparkled with dew, animals grazed in groups near the road, or walked in leisurely fashion back from the river. Sometimes Emma would pull off the tar and into one of the little slip roads that gave a closer view of the river. Here she would stop the car and look through the trees on to the river bank. Sometimes there was game. Often there was not. But always the sandy banks were covered with the imprints of thousands of footmarks – impala, monkeys, warthogs, and giraffe. She wished she could tell the animals by their footprints, wished she knew which creatures had walked here. Stewart, she thought, would know.

When the sun stood higher in the sky and she was beginning to feel peckish and warm, Emma would wend her way back to camp and there, after shedding her jerseys and putting on a blouse and shorts, she would make herself breakfast.

The constant holiday feeling, the informality of her new life, these were a constant joy to her. Standing with other women at a fire, she would fry eggs and a little bacon, and often after a second cup of coffee, she would pop into the shop or the office for a few minutes. A few minutes of conversation with Lance made a pleasant interlude. Then back to her hut, out with the map to plan the day's driving, and with cameras and field glasses and a little fruit, away she would go once more.

In the distance, sometimes, she caught a glimpse of a tall lean figure in a safari suit, but though they said hello once or twice, when they met, their contact was limited, and Emma believed she was glad of it. It was turning out easier than she had feared to keep things uncomplicated.

One morning she went into the shop and stood thoughtfully at the bookstall. 'Looking for something in particular?' asked one of the assistants who had come to know her.

'Actually, yes, I thought you might have a book showing the different types of game. It seems ridiculous,' she made a helpless gesture with her hands, 'but I see so many beautiful buck and birds and never know their names. Is there such a book?'

'Why, yes, of course,' said the girl, picking up a few books and handing them to Emma. 'This one is pretty good. This one too. Why not look through them and see what you fancy?'

Emma had chosen two books and was just taking out her purse to pay for them when a voice behind her said, 'I could help you if you like.'

She looked around and saw a young boy behind her. He said again, 'I could help you, if you like.'

'In what way could you help me?' she asked gently.

'I heard what you were saying about the animals. I could come in your car with you and tell you their names.' He was about twelve years old, sandy-haired and freckled, his feet bare and his hands thrust into the pockets of his shorts in an imitation of a grown-up. His lower lip was caught between his teeth as he looked up at her. Then he asked again, 'Would you like that?'

'Why, do you know so much about animals?' Emma asked him.

'This is Johnny.' The assistant coming up with the change just then had heard the interchange, and smiled down at the boy. 'Johnny is the son of one of the game rangers. He'll tell you all you want to know.'

'That would be absolutely lovely. I'm going out in about ten minutes, Johnny. If you really want to come with me, though, I think you should go and tell your mother first.'

Soon they were turning out of the big gates, and in a few minutes they were talking like old friends.

'I can show you a super road, Miss Anderson,' said Johnny.

'I'd like that. But won't you call me, Emma, Johnny? Then I'll really feel that we're going to be friends.'

'Okay. Emma . . .' Johnny said it slowly, trying out the sound of the name so thoughtfully that Emma had to suppress a laugh.

'Emma. I've hardly ever heard that name before, but it's nice,' he said at last.

'I'm glad you like it,' she said, laughing. 'All right, Johnny, lead the way.' And turning the car in the direction he suggested, she began to drive along a road she had not seen before.

'Do you live in the Park, then?' she asked presently.

'Yes. My dad's a ranger.'

'What about school?'

'Oh, I go to school in town. But it's holidays right now.' He looked at her thoughtfully. 'What do you do?'

'At the moment I'm here to take pictures for a book someone's writing.'

'But you don't know much about animals, do you?'

'I'm hoping I'll learn.' She laughed again, enjoying his directness. 'Would you like to teach me?'

'Sure. That's why I came with you.'

'Fibber!'

'Honest.' He stared at her with eyes that were too wide.

'You mean you only came because you wanted to teach me about the animals?' Her eyes twinkled as she looked away from the road and into his face. 'It's awfully nice to have you with me, Johnny. But why, really, did you want to come?'

'Okay,' he said with an air of resignation. 'It's because you looked nice and I wanted to go for a drive. My dad takes me with him whenever he can, but sometimes he can't, and most of the term I'm stuck away at school, so on a super day like today I couldn't just hang around the

34

camp, could I?'

'Of course you couldn't. What are you going to be when you grow up, Johnny?'

'Oh . . .' He looked away uncertainly.

'A ranger like your father?'

'Yes – No. Well, actually . . .' He paused a moment looking at her intently as if trying to make up his mind about something. At last he said, 'You won't laugh if I tell you?'

'Of course not.'

'Well . . .' He sat forward, hunching his chin into his hands. 'I'd like to live here, be a ranger like my dad . . . but also there's something I want to do as well.'

'And what is that?' Emma found herself becoming really interested in the child.

'I want to be an artist.'

'An artist?' Emma exclaimed, astonished. 'You like to paint, Johnny?'

'I love it. I love it more than anything else. And I love the animals and the bush. So you see, if I lived here and became a ranger, I could look after animals *and* paint them.'

'The best of both worlds,' Emma smiled, looking at the child beside her. The tousled hair and the bare feet, the faded shorts and the T-shirt with a picture of a cross-eyed sailor on it. Who would have thought the soul of an artist dwelt beneath that picture?

'Will you show me your work one day?' she asked him.

'Sure, if you really want to see it.'

'Oh, I do.'

'Well, sure, then. And would you like to show me *your* pictures?'

'I'd like to,' she said seriously, one artist speaking to another. 'When I've had some developed. Though of course what you do is much more difficult. I only have to click the camera – you have to paint the whole picture.'

'Sure.' He thought about it. 'I guess that's so. Still, you do see some super photos sometimes.'

'Yes. Oh, look,' she said suddenly, as a tiny animal sprang from the side of the road into the bush. 'Is that an impala? I've seen those before and wasn't certain.'

'That's a duiker,' he told her.

'Oh!'

'There aren't as many of them.'

'I always think of all buck as impala, but they're not, are they?'

He looked at her so thoughtfully that she had to force herself to keep her face serious, expecting he would come out with some mocking rejoinder, but he only said, perfectly seriously,'You really don't know very much about buck, do you?'

'I'm afraid not.'

'Well, look, I'm not busy every day. There are days when I don't go out with my dad. So I really think I should spend some time with you and teach you about the animals. I mean, you'll have to know more than you do for your book, won't you?'

'I'd really appreciate it if you would do that,' Emma said gratefully.

'I suppose you know most of the game rangers?' she said a little while later as she drove slowly, keeping her eyes fixed to her side of the road.

'A good many.'

'Do you know a man called Stewart?' she said casually.

'Sure. Stewart's great. He's my pal.' The boy's voice was warm with admiration. 'Do *you* know him?'

'I've – spoken to him once or twice.'

'Yes, well, the thing about Stewart is . . .' He broke off,

maddeningly, at this point. 'Look, Emma, there's a water-buck.'

She stopped the car and looked into the bush. 'Where? I can't see a thing ... Oh, Johnny, you're having me on!'

'Look,' he said patiently, pointing. 'There! I think it's coming this way.'

'Oh, there! Oh, Johnny, I see it. Is that really a water-buck?'

'Yes, that's what it is.'

'How can you tell?' she asked.

'See that white circle around the back of his body?'

'Yes.'

'That's what my science teacher would call a distinctive feature.'

'You're really awfully clever, Johnny,' she said admiringly.

'Thank you,' he said quite seriously. 'And I think you're pretty nice.'

The compliment was so much from the heart that Emma turned in her seat and gave him a brief hug.

'Aw,' he said awkwardly, 'I just wish ladies didn't always feel they have to kiss and hug. Still, you *are* nice. Have you got any friends besides me and Stewart?'

'Stewart isn't really a friend, Johnny. I've just spoken to him a few times, that's all. And then there's Lance – he works in the shop. Do you know him?'

'Yes.'

'Is he one of your pals too?'

'No.'

'Oh.'

'He and Stewart don't like each other,' Johnny explained.

'Oh ... they don't?'

'No.'

Emma longed to ask more, but Johnny was little more than a child, and though she knew she could have found a way of making her questions seem quite innocent, she felt she would in some way be taking advantage of the situation.

Slowly they drove along, and when Johnny was not telling her about the various animals and birds they saw, he told her about the trees and bushes and the wild flowers that grew near the river. She was astonished at the wideness of his knowledge, and listened quietly to his talk, enjoying the mixture of schoolboy enthusiasm and wild-life expertise, through all of which ran his great love for the Park.

'Will you let me buy you a cool drink?' she asked him when they were back at Skukuza, and she was parking her car under a wide flowering tree, alive with the hum of bees.

'Well . . . I don't know,' he began.

'It's so hot, Johnny. If I don't have something nice and cool I'll just melt away, and I don't feel like sitting alone.'

'Well, I don't know what my mom will say . . .' All at once, back at camp, he was conscious of her status as a tourist, and was shy.

'I thought we were pals,' Emma protested.

'We are. Of course we are.'

'Well then?'

'It's just . . .' he hesitated.

'That I'm a visitor. But I'm going to be here quite a while, so couldn't you try to think of me as just half a visitor?'

'I suppose I could,' he shrugged.

'Good. I'll go and sit down and while I order – what would you like, by the way? – won't you bring me some of your paintings? I would so much like to see them.'

38

Fifteen minutes later they sat side by side, sipping iced drinks from long glasses, while Emma leafed through a file of pictures.

'This is beautiful, Johnny.' She had stopped at a picture of a kudu, the magnificent animal that Johnny had mentioned earlier was one of his favourite subjects.

'It's not bad.' His face shone with pleasure at her praise, though he tried hard to pretend modesty.

'I think it's outstanding. You've caught the whole character of the animal.' She was silent as she studied it more carefully. Do you remember when we saw the kudu come out of the bushes? I was thinking how very regal it looked. Like a kind of royal buck. And you've caught it all.'

'I have?' The boy squirmed with joy.

'Those lovely horns, and the graceful way it holds its head, and even . . .'

'I see you've discovered our artist.' Emma and Johnny looked up. Standing behind the boy, one hand resting affectionately on his shoulder, was Stewart. He was smiling, looking tall and bronzed and very relaxed, and unexpectedly Emma's heart skipped a beat.

'Won't you join us?' she heard herself saying.

'Thank you. Though that sweet frothy stuff you folks are drinking is not quite my style.' He beckoned to one of the waiters and ordered a beer. 'And now,' he turned back to Emma, 'what do you think of Johnny?'

'He's excellent, isn't he?'

'I think he's going to be one of the wild-life artists of our day,' Stewart said quietly. He smiled at the boy and when Johnny smiled back Emma saw the bond of affection and understanding that existed between them. 'We're going to be very proud of Johnny one day.'

'Oh, Stewart!' The boy did not know how to hide his joy.

'And how did the two of you get to know each other?'

Before Emma could reply Johnny had told Stewart of the meeting in the shop and of the drive they had taken together. 'Do you know, she doesn't know a water-buck from an eland or an impala?' he told Stewart.

'I'm sure she'll learn with your very able guidance,' Stewart grinned.

'Oh, yes, we're going to be friends.' There was an engaging sweetness about the child, though Emma knew he would be embarrassed to hear it.

'Well, that's good,' Stewart said. 'I'm pleased.'

'Dad wouldn't let me go with him today,' Johnny looked up from his cool drink.

'I know. He's out looking for snares.'

'Are there poachers about again?'

'It seems like it.' Stewart turned to Emma. 'One of our perennial headaches.'

'Is that why I couldn't go with him?' Johnny's face puckered in a frown.

'You know how it is when you're dealing with poachers. There could be trouble.'

'When I'm big I'll . . .' Johnny made a fearsome-looking gesture, drawing his hand rapidly past his neck. 'Then they won't come back.'

'Good. I hope you'll scare the daylights out of them.' Stewart drained the last of his beer and got up to go. 'Well, folks, I enjoyed that. Have to make tracks now.' He smiled down at Emma. 'Perhaps if you have time to spare and this youngster lets you off the rein, you might like to come for a drive with me one of these days?'

'Thank you, I'd like that.' Emma watched him walk away, hoping the radiance she felt did not shine too clearly in her eyes for all to see.

CHAPTER THREE

A DAY or two later Emma stood at the fence by the river, searching the bush for game. It was a lovely day. It had rained during the night, and though she knew it would soon be as hot as it always was, there was a newly-washed radiance about the countryside. Soon she would go back to her hut, fetch her cameras and start out for the day. But for the moment she was enjoying, as she always did, the sounds of camp life behind her, the drone of the bees in the trees, the endless vista that stretched before her.

'This place draws you like a magnet, doesn't it?' She looked up into Lance's smiling eyes.

'It *is* beautiful,' she smiled back.

'It is,' he agreed. 'And isn't it lucky I'm beginning to know your favourite haunts? I was looking for you.'

'Oh, were you, Lance?' Since the braai Lance had been on duty at what he termed 'all the most awkward times', and though whenever Emma saw him in the shop or the office they exchanged a joke or a few words, they had not had the chance to spend much time together.

'I'm free today,' he was saying. 'Well, actually, I should be on duty, but I managed to work a point. It *is* Sunday, after all. Will you spend the day with me, Emma?'

'You're not on duty, then?'

'One of the other chaps agreed to change shifts.'

'Persuasive character,' she laughed.

'Persuasive enough to coax you into fetching your swimsuit and coming out for the day with me?'

'Swimsuit?' she asked, mystified.

'I thought we'd take a drive to Pretoriuskop. There's a pool there. You do have a swimsuit, don't you?'

'Fortunately, yes.'

'You must see Pretoriuskop. And today is perfect. It's going to be a scorcher again, just right for a dip.'

'You've persuaded me,' she said, laughing.

'Good girl. When will you be ready to go?'

'I must go back to my room for a few minutes. Shall I meet you at your car in a quarter of an hour?'

'So long?' For some unknown reason he looked anxious. 'Couldn't you be quicker?'

'I'll try,' she promised, wondering as she began to walk to her hut why he was in such a hurry. It was still early and the day stretched before them. And then, as she approached her door, the question fled her mind, for Stewart and Johnny stood there waiting.

'Stewart! Johnny!' she called happily. 'It's good to see you.'

'We thought we'd wait for you here,' Stewart said, smiling. 'Johnny's idea. He went to see if your car was still in the car-park, and as it was he guessed you'd come this way sooner or later.'

'And here I am,' she smiled.

'And here you are. How would you like to come out for the the the day with us?'

'Today?' All at once the brightness of the day seemed to have dulled.

'It's Sunday,' said Stewart. 'I'm free, and Johnny and I thought we'd take you for a drive, have lunch at Lower Sabie and take a slow drive back in the afternoon.'

'I . . . I can't,' she faltered.

'No?' Stewart looked at her curiously.

'But why not?' Johnny burst out.

'A few minutes ago I saw Lance, and he asked me to spend the day with him. He wants to go to Pretoriuskop . . . He asked me to fetch my swimsuit and . . .'

'You can't go with Lance!' Johnny wailed.

'I'm afraid I promised.'

Johnny's brow was wrinkled in a frown. 'Stewart,' he said, 'when you and I were talking in the shop just now ... when you said we could ask Emma to come with us ... Did you see Lance?'

'He may have been around,' Stewart agreed.

'He was right there, next to us.'

'Perhaps he was. I don't remember.'

'But I do. Because I remember he was trying to open a case of cold drinks and was having trouble. And Stewart, he was trying to listen to what we were saying.'

'Don't let your imagination run away with you, Johnny.'

'He was, Stewart. I know he was!'

'Perhaps you're right.' Stewart's face was impassive as he looked at Emma. 'But that doesn't change anything, does it?'

'I promised,' she said unhappily. 'Besides – oh, Johnny, you're wrong. I know you are.'

'But he *was* there. I remember.'

'Well, of course he was there. He works in the shop,' reasoned Emma.

'He was listening to us.'

'Careful, Johnny,' Stewart cautioned.

'But I know he was! I remember now. He stayed near us to hear what we were saying.'

'I can't believe that, Johnny,' said Emma. 'Lance isn't like that. You don't like him. But he really *is* a nice man.'

'But I tell you ...' The child's face was angry, and he looked close to tears.

'Whatever the truth of it may be,' Stewart said quietly, 'we mustn't keep Emma talking like this. She's going out for the day, and there's someone waiting for her.'

Emma would have given anything at that moment to

say, 'I want nothing more than to spend the day with you both. I could make an excuse to Lance.' But she knew she could not do it. It would be like stabbing the man in the back. And for all Johnny said about him, he had shown her nothing but friendliness.

'There's not much I can do about it now,' she began.

'Of course not.' Stewart smiled suddenly. 'You're merely paying the penalty for being too popular.'

'It's quite a predicament, isn't it?'

'Not at all. Lance asked you first. You accepted, and you must go with him.'

'That's right.' She looked at him gratefully. Then she ventured, 'Perhaps we could make it another day, Stewart?'

'We'll do that,' he promised. 'Come, Johnny, let's see what you and I can make of the day by ourselves.'

Emma was thoughtful as she took her things and went to meet Lance. It was nonsense, of course, what Johnny was suggesting. Lance couldn't help being in the shop. It was, after all, the place where he worked, where he was supposed to be. But she remembered what he had said about getting somebody to change shifts with him. Was it possible that he had only invited her because of what he had heard?

His face appeared before her eyes – the handsome, laughing face with the even-teethed smile. Oh, it was nonsense, sheer nonsense. In his disappointment Johnny had talked himself into something. Even Stewart had not allowed him to pursue the point. After all, Lance *had* told her that he had changed shifts. It was not as though he had tried to lie about that. And his explanation had been perfectly reasonable.

She must remember the resolution she had made. All men were going to be completely equal in her affections. Stewart and Lance had their own reasons for not liking

44

each other, reasons that did not concern her. She was going to enjoy the day, and that was that.

Lance was waiting for her, and as she approached the car and saw him standing there, handsome and smiling, she knew with a sudden sinking of the heart, in spite of her resolution, that all men could never be equal in her affections.

'That was quick,' he said, and for a moment she wondered whether he sounded too hearty. 'It's going to be a super day, Emma. I just know it.'

'I know it too.' She smiled at him, apologizing to him silently for having doubted him. 'Heavens, it really is turning into another scorcher. It will be lovely to have a dip.'

Lance was good company. Stewart could be caustic when the mood took him, but Lance seemed to be always relaxed and smiling, eager to please and give her a good time. While they drove he told her anecdotes about the people who lived and worked in the camp, many of whom she had already met. Sometimes the stories he told her were a little malicious, but they were so amusing, and told with such good nature, that it was difficult not to laugh at them.

Stewart was the only person Lance did not mention, and Emma was glad. Instinctively she knew that she did not want to hear any barbed anecdotes about him. And even if the story were to be completely without any sting she still did not want to hear it.

When they arrived at Pretoriuskop Lance took her to the restaurant for a cool drink. Emma could see that this camp, the oldest of all camps in the game reserve, was quite different from Skukuza. She came to realize eventually, when she had seen more of the park, that each camp had an atmosphere and character of its own. There was no river at Pretoriuskop, but as they sat at the restaurant, under the trees, sipping their drinks, Emma looked about her and thought how peaceful and pretty it was.

Presently they walked to the swimming-pool, and Emma changed into her swimsuit. Lance was looking at her with such frank admiration when she joined him that she covered up her embarrassment by saying, 'I hadn't realized how burnt I'd become. And so lopsided too. I suppose it's because I'm always driving, so the arm on the driving side is more tanned than the other.'

'You look lovely. You must have had many boy-friends back home, Emma.'

She was silent, remembering Jimmy, of whom she was beginning to think less and less often. 'One or two,' she said at length.

'You're very beautiful, Emma.'

'Thank you,' she said, feeling herself flush beneath his gaze.

'Has Stewart told you that you're beautiful?'

'Oh, for heaven's sake!'

'Has he, Emma?' Lance insisted.

'No,' she said quietly, 'Stewart hasn't said I'm beautiful. There's really no reason why he should have. Let's change the subject, Lance. We were having such a lovely day. I'd hate to spoil it.'

'Of course,' he said. Getting up abruptly, he walked to the edge of the pool, and rising lightly on to his toes dived into the water.

Emma watched as he swam across the pool. He had an easy effortless style that was a pleasure to see. He swam four lengths without stopping, and then he waved to her to come in too. Cupping his hands around his mouth he called, 'Lazybones! Come in before I drag you in!' Emma was so glad to see that he had recovered his good humour that she walked to the edge of the pool, sat down on the side, and gingerly dipped in a toe. 'Don't!' she shouted when he came near and threw water at her. 'That's awful!'

'Come in, then.' He moved his hands under the water in a playful threat as if he intended splashing her again, but before he could do so she slithered into the water. 'Oh, it's freezing!' she gasped. 'Absolutely freezing!'

'It's gorgeous. Swim, and you'll be warm.'

She swam twice across the pool, conscious of his eyes upon her, and glad that she had had lessons when she was small, so that her style was not all that bad. 'You're right,' she said, swimming up to him, 'it *is* gorgeous. I wish we could stay in the water all day.'

Lance looked at her as she swam up to him. Suddenly he put a hand on each side of her wet face, and for a moment they were both quite still, looking at each other. 'You really are very beautiful,' he said, bending his own wet face to hers, as he kissed her lightly on the lips. Then he dropped his hands and swam away.

After a while Emma began to feel chilly, and she climbed out of the pool. She took a towel, rubbed it across her back and shoulders, then spread it on the lawn and lay down to sunbathe. Lance stayed in the water a little longer, then he too came out, towelled himself dry, stretched out beside her and fell asleep. The kiss was not mentioned between them.

They left Pretoriuskop soon after lunch. In terms of miles it was not far to Skukuza, but as they drove so slowly, distances in the Park took a long time to cover. And besides, as Emma had discovered for herself by now, if you drove at the maximum speed limit the chances were that you would miss animals that were not actually at the roadside.

The sun was setting when they drove into the gates of Skukuza. 'It's been a lovely day,' Emma said warmly. 'A lovely, lovely day.'

'I'm glad you enjoyed it.' The expression on his face

was so enigmatic that she wondered what he was thinking. 'We must do it again.'

She noticed then that he was looking fixedly at a car in
the car-park, and following the direction of his eyes she
saw that he was looking at a little red car that was parked
nearby. 'I see Stewart's girl-friend has come to visit him,'
he said at length.

'Stewart's girl-friend?' she echoed foolishly.

'She visits him sometimes. She stays in town, and every
now and then she comes up for a few days. She's – mad
about Stewart.'

'But . . .' Emma could feel her hands trembling and
hoped Lance wouldn't notice. 'I don't understand . . . Stewart couldn't have known she was coming today.'

'And why couldn't he have known?'

'Because . . . because he asked me to spend the day with
him, after you'd already asked me . . . and if he'd known
she was coming he wouldn't have done that.'

'Perhaps it's because he knew she was coming that he
asked you.' Lance was watching her intently now.

'He wouldn't have done that,' she said slowly.

'No? Well,' Lance chuckled, 'Stewart's a strange one.
Remember, I wanted you not to go breaking your heart
over him.'

'I don't intend breaking my heart over anyone – I told
you that once before. But I still don't see why Stewart
would ask me to come out with him when he knew his . . .
when he knew he was having a visitor.'

'Could be he was trying to make her jealous.' Lance's
voice held a strange tinge of bitterness. 'Miranda is a
beautiful woman. A very beautiful woman.'

'Oh!' Emma felt a little sick, wondering how to end
the conversation.

'Like to have supper with me?' she heard Lance saying.

'Oh, no, Lance, thank you. I'm feeling a little tired. All

that sun, you know . . . and the water. I think I'll just go to bed.' She forced a smile. 'Thank you again for a lovely day.'

She was walking to her hut when she saw them. Miranda was indeed a beautiful woman. She was older than Emma, at least thirty, and so nearer in age to Stewart than Emma was, and even at this distance she could see that she possessed poise and charm.

Long glossy black hair framed a perfectly-featured oval face. She was looking up at Stewart and he was bending slightly to hear what she was saying. Emma could not see the expression on Stewart's face, but she could see the radiance that shone in Miranda's smile. Something she said must have amused Stewart, for she heard him chuckle as he bent towards her and gave her a quick hug.

Emma did not wait to see more. She was just grateful that they had not seen her. She turned quickly and stumbled blindly up to her hut.

When she got there she found she was not hungry, and after making herself a cup of coffee, she lay on her bed.

She hardly noticed the time as the sunset turned into darkness, so absorbed was she in her thoughts. Had both men had their own reasons for wanting her company that day? Johnny had implied that Lance had only wanted her to accompany him as a means of spiting Stewart. And if Lance was right about Stewart, if Stewart had really known his girl-friend was coming, and, really, how could he not have known, why had he asked her to come with him? Was it to make Miranda jealous?

Strangely, though the thought of Lance using her for his own ends made her angry, it was the idea that Stewart had lied to her that was unendurable. But why this was so she was not yet ready to admit to herself.

She was walking through the camp next morning when she saw them together again. The girl was talking in an animated voice and when she smiled at Stewart Emma saw again the radiance in her face. This time, before she could avoid them, Stewart saw her.

'Emma!' he called. 'Hello. I want you to meet Miranda.' He turned to the girl at his side. 'Miranda, this is Emma. She's come to live here for a while.'

Emma saw the girl look at her appraisingly. 'Are you on the staff?' she asked.

'No. I'm here to take pictures.'

'Pictures?' Miranda queried.

'Photographs,' Emma explained. 'For a book.'

'Then you won't be here long?'

'About three months.'

'Ah, how nice.'

'Lance has been showing Emma around,' Stewart told Miranda. 'And I've also been giving her the odd bit of advice. And warning,' he added, grinning at Emma.

'You're very lucky to have found yourself such good guides.' Again Miranda smiled, but Emma saw the hostility in her face, there was a keep-your-hands-off-my-property look that she recognized.

'Well, anyway . . .' she smiled at them both, 'I'm going out driving now. Nice to have met you, Miranda.'

So this was Stewart's girl-friend, she thought as she drove slowly and unseeingly. Close to, she was even lovelier than from afar. 'I don't know why that should depress me,' Emma told herself sternly. 'I decided I wasn't going to let any man mean anything more than a friend. So why should it matter if a girl is here to visit Stewart? He can have a hundred girls if he wants to, I'm sure, arrogant and sure of himself as he is. It really doesn't matter to me at all.' But in her heart she knew that it did matter. It was beginning to matter too much.

It was foolish of her not to have realized that a man like Stewart, alone and in his early thirties, must have a woman in his life. All at once she caught herself wishing that she was older than her twenty-two years. If only she were dark and poised and charming and sophisticated — like . . . like Miranda.

'You're not going to refuse me today.' It was a morning a few days later, and Emma forced herself to turn slowly and look up into Stewart's face. Then she turned back to the river.

'Refuse you what?'

'I'm going to Lower Sabie today,' he said. 'I want you to come with me.'

'Oh!'

'I know you love that view, Emma. It's the only place I know I can find you. But do you think you could look at me and give me an answer?'

'Of all the . . .' She turned to him angrily, but then paused as he smiled, and she felt her heart turn over.

'We're not going to quarrel, are we? I was only joking.'

'I know.'

'And you will come with me today?'

Yes, yes, yes, she wanted to shout. Of course I'll come with you, and I don't care what Miranda or Lance or anybody else cares to think. This is what I want to do and I will do it. 'Yes,' she smiled, 'I'd like that.'

'Funny how things sometimes turn out for the best,' he said musingly. 'When I asked you to come out with Johnny and me the other day I didn't know Miranda was coming up.'

'You didn't?' she couldn't help saying.

'Well, of course not, you silly little thing,' he said gently. 'That would have been a foolish thing for me to

51

do if I had known.'

The subject of Miranda was not one she wanted to dwell on, but there was relief in her that he had mentioned it. It showed that Stewart had not been playing her up against the other girl when he had made his invitation.

All at once she knew she could relax in his company. Stewart had asked her out on Sunday because it was what he had wanted to do, and not for any ulterior motive. Miranda existed. She was a factor in his life. But that had nothing to do with her, Emma. If Stewart wanted to take her for a drive she was content to go with him, and that, for the moment, was all that mattered.

The Lower Sabie Road seemed to have a special radiance that day. Every now and then Stewart would stop the car to point out animals to her, and she realized how very much she did not know.

So many things had special relevance for Stewart – footprints in the sand beside the road, movement in the bushes, a flight of birds or the turn of an impala's head. Johnny had impressed her with his knowledge, and Lance certainly seemed to know a little about animals, but when Stewart spoke it was the confidence and knowledge and authority of a man who lives and knows the creatures of the wild that shone through his words.

At one point he turned off on to a slip road that led down almost to the banks of the river. He stopped the car beneath a shady tree with low overhanging branches. Emma wound down her window and breathed deeply of the fragrant air.

All around it was quiet and peaceful and very beautiful. The sun shone and sparkled on the water, the sandbank sloped gently down to the water, pockmarked with the feet of a thousand animals who had used this bank to drink from and in the branches overhead an exotic bird uttered a harsh shrill sound. Then all was still.

'Don't you know you should never have your window open?' Stewart was smiling.

'But there's nothing here. Oh, I forgot,' Emma laughed. 'There's a lion behind that bush.'

'No, there's no lion. But you never know when there might be.'

'But you've got eyes on all sides of your head and wouldn't let me come to any harm, would you?'

'No, Emma, I would never let you come to harm.' The words were spoken quietly, but even though she knew they held no special relevance her heart seemed to leap.

'It's so lovely here,' she said, to change the subject. 'Do you know what I'd really like to do?'

'Let's hear.'

'Lie on those rocks and sunbathe.' When he let out a roar of laughter she pretended to pout and said, 'Obviously I wouldn't be so foolish, but even you can't tell me there's a lion out there.'

'No lion, no.' He was still laughing. 'But look carefully. See anything?'

She narrowed her eyes and searched the trees, the river, the rocks, for sign of an animal. At last she turned back to him. 'You're teasing me.'

'You think so?'

'Perhaps there's a mouse in the bushes, but I could find one even in England.'

'You could?' he asked in pretended astonishment.

'And what's more, I'm not afraid of mice,' she added firmly.

'I'm very glad to hear it.' He laughed again, and the sound of it was music in her ears. 'So, Emma, you'd be perfectly happy to go and sunbathe on those nice broad rocks?'

There must be something on those rocks – he seemed so obsessed with them. Carefully Emma searched every inch of them with her eyes, but there was nothing to be seen. 'Some kind of poisonous lizard hiding out there?' she suggested at length.

This time he let out a roar of laughter. 'Something like that.' He reached behind him, took her binoculars from the back seat and handed them to her. 'Put those to your eyes and look again.'

She glanced at him suspiciously as she took them from him. Even while she enjoyed this lighthearted mood of his she was not certain whether she could trust it. 'All right,' she said, lifting the binoculars to her eyes and trying to focus on the rocks. 'Let's see this fearsome animal of yours.'

At first she could only see bits of greenery and branches, but at last the glasses seemed to be trained on the right spot. It took her a moment to get used to the sight and then – 'Stewart!' It was a horrified gasp. 'Oh, Stewart!'

'I take it that means you've spotted the poisonous lizard?' he chuckled.

'Oh, Stewart!' she said for the third time, and then, lowering the binoculars, she looked at him dazed. 'Is . . . is that really a crocodile?'

'It really is,' he said quietly, and all the laughter had vanished from his eyes.

She looked at it again without the glasses, before lifting them to her eyes once more. 'It's incredible!'

'It is rather, isn't it?'

'So enormous. And I thought it was a rock. From here it looks just like all the other rocks. I never dreamed a crocodile could be so big.'

She lifted the glasses to her eyes again, mesmerized by the hideous prehistoric-looking animal. 'It's so still. It doesn't move. It isn't dead, is it?'

'Oh, no, it isn't dead.'

'It's so completely motionless.'

'It could stay like that for hours, Emma. You could watch it for hours and never see it move.'

'Is it sleeping?' she asked.

Stewart laughed quietly. 'No, it's wide awake — very wide awake. If a tasty morsel were to arrive you'd see a wild threshing of tail, and the poor creature that didn't see the crocodile would be no more.'

'Does it happen often?'

'Unfortunately. It's so easy to mistake a crocodile for a rock.'

'It looks just like one. All those grey rocks on either side of it. I really thought it was a rock too.'

'That's right,' he agreed.

'It's uncanny,' she mused, 'that an animal can blend so absolutely with its surroundings.'

'Camouflage. Have you noticed how many of the animals blend with the bushes and the sand? That's their form of natural protection.'

'There's so much to know, isn't there?' she said.

'If you mean camouflage alone — that isn't all that difficult. But the animals as such, their ways and how they live — yes, there is a lot.'

'You love it, don't you?' she said impulsively.

'It's my life,' he said, looking quietly over the river.

'There's nothing else you want?'

'I wouldn't say that.' He turned his gaze and looked steadily into her eyes. 'There *are* things I want. No man is entirely self-sufficient and content, is he? But my life is here, with the animals, and I would like to think that — the other things I want could fit in with the existing scheme of things.'

Her eyes dropped beneath his. She was a little uncertain what he meant.

'Why have you come here?' Stewart asked.

'To take photos. You know that.'

'There's another reason, isn't there?'

'Is it so obvious?' she asked at last, painfully.

'You know so little about animals, and not all that very much about photography.' His voice was so gentle that she could not possibly take offence at what he was saying. 'Sometimes it helps to talk. One sees things in better perspective. If that's the way it would be with you ... would you like to tell me?'

'His name was Jimmy,' she said at last, and her voice was low and a little unsteady. 'We'd been going around together for some time. We were getting married. I was so happy.' She was quiet for a while, and he didn't press her to go on. 'It was all arranged. The dress was being made and the flowers had been ordered. We'd been looking around for a flat. It wasn't easy to find anything – we couldn't afford much. Jimmy ... Jimmy was clever, an engineer. He wasn't earning much yet, but he had plans – such wonderful plans ...'

'And then?' he prompted her gently.

'The man he worked for had a daughter, and she liked Jimmy. He was so handsome – handsome and clever and fun. He would have made his way to the top. It would have taken time, but he'd have got there.'

'He saw a quicker way?'

'I don't think it was that way at the beginning. He used to laugh about it sometimes. The way she'd wait for him when he was coming out of the building, and ask him to go places with her. But then ... well, after a while he didn't laugh about it, and if I made a joke it didn't seem funny.'

'He couldn't have fallen in love with her,' said Stewart.

56

'I think he liked her. It's so easy to like someone who likes you. And then her father ... He promised Jimmy so much. Jimmy was clever and her father didn't want to lose him. He promised him a partnership in his company, and a lovely house, and ... and other things.'

'If Jimmy was so clever wouldn't he have got to the top anyway?'

'He would, I know he would have. But it was quicker this way. Jimmy was so ambitious. We began to quarrel. In the end ... in the end I think he was very happy for us to break up.'

'And the break-up came just a month before your wedding?'

'Yes.'

'It must have been tough for you,' Stewart commented.

'I cried,' she confessed. 'I didn't know I had it in me to cry so hard. For two days I cried. I didn't eat, and my mother worried that I would get sick.'

'What did Jimmy do when he heard?'

'He never knew,' Emma said quietly. 'I wouldn't let them phone him. It would have done no good in the end. I understood that at least.'

'He must have been a fool to let you go.' Again he looked at her with the quiet gaze that made her heart skip a beat. 'So that's why you came here?'

'I had to get away – away from England, from all the unhappiness. The ship sailed the day we were to have been married. A friend of my father's, a very close friend, is a wild-life enthusiast, and he knew what had happened. He's been here and is writing a book about his experiences. He suggested that if I wanted to come here to take pictures of the animals – photography really is my hobby – he would be happy to use them.'

'I see ...'

'Life goes on, doesn't it?' She turned to look at him, although she knew that her eyes were wet. 'Sometimes it's so tough that you think you can never pull yourself together again. But things go on.'

'Yes.' He moved towards her, put an arm around her shoulders and held her close. 'Life goes on. It has to.' After a moment he said, 'I've learnt that too.'

Emma looked at him questioningly without speaking. It gave her a strange sense of comfort to sit with him like this. It had been a purely platonic gesture, she knew, when he had put his arm around her. It was a gesture intended to comfort and warm, and it had succeeded in its purpose.

'I was married once,' he said very slowly. 'Did you know that?'

She shook her head wordlessly, and felt a little knife of disappointment and anguish twist inside her.

'Her name was Mary, and we lived in one of the game parks further north. Not this sort of thing that we have here, camps with huts and facilities for visitors. We had a little cottage, all alone in the midst of an enormous stretch of land.'

'It must have been lonely.'

'It didn't seem so – then,' he said.

'Where – where is Mary now?' she forced herself to ask.

'She was killed.'

'Oh, Stewart! Oh, no!'

'It was something that should never have happened,' he said steadily. His arm was still around her shoulders, but she sensed that his mind was far away, with Mary, in that distant game park. 'She – she was killed by a lion. It shouldn't have happened, but she broke a rule – one of the cardinal rules that anyone living in the bush, as we did, should have kept to. Afterwards . . .' She thought she heard a break in his voice. 'Afterwards, when it was all over, I left our home. I couldn't bear to be there any more – alone. I came here.'

'Oh, Stewart! It's so dreadful! I don't know what to say.'

'There's nothing you can say. I'll never forget her, of course. I don't think you can ever forget a person you've loved. But I've got over it. It's taken a long time. But I've got over it.'

'And I thought what happened to me was bad.' She looked up at him and now she was crying. 'I feel so ashamed.'

'Emma,' he leaned towards her and kissed her very gently, 'everything is relative. Whatever happens means a lot to the person it happens to at the time that it happens.'

'And yet . . .'

'You've had your tough time. What happened to you is hard for any girl to accept, but you'll get over it. You've made the first step, haven't you?'

'Yes, I've made the first step,' she said, and she smiled at him.

'Good.' He took his arm from her shoulders. 'Keep it up. And to help you I'll take you to a spot where the animals come to drink, and where you can sit with your camera for hours and perhaps manage to get a few really good shots.'

It was a lovely spot, this place that Stewart took her to. A little clearing by the river, similar to the one where they had been sitting, but with an uninterrupted view of the river-bank, and of the little paths that the animals had made with their daily walk to the river and back to drink. It was a place which Emma could never have found by herself, a ranger's slip road which Stewart gave her permission to use whenever she wanted to.

Here, she knew, she could sit for hours, with her camera by her side, absorbing the peace and beauty into her mind and nerve-stream, and all the while she would be ready to take photographs whenever the opportunity arose.

'Thank you,' she said, turning to him impulsively. 'Oh, thank you, Stewart.'

'Like it?' He was looking at her with an expression that held something in it that she could not quite put a name to.

'It's heaven! It's like a piece of paradise planted on earth.'

'I'm so glad.' He put the car into gear and turned it back in the direction of the road.

She was disappointed. 'Are we going already?'

'You can come here any time you want to. But I must get on to Lower Sabie. If I don't get there soon the man I want to speak to will think I'm not coming. Besides,' he grinned at her mischievously, 'soon that tummy of yours is going to start grumbling for its food!'

They came at last to Lower Sabie. Stewart stopped the car for a few minutes outside the gates before driving in. Just beyond the camp stood a big water tower, and all over it swarmed scores of the little grey vervet monkeys. They swung from the steel girders, jumping, playing, pulling at each other's tails, swooping down and then reaching up again, and looking as if at any moment they would fall.

'They're gorgeous,' Emma laughed. 'The lion may be the king around here, but he's so lazy, always playing so hard to get. These little creatures make me laugh.'

'The kids love them too,' Stewart told her. 'I think the highlight of many a child's day is if his dad drives a mile or two with a monkey clinging to his carrier.'

They drove into the camp, and when Stewart had parked the car he said, 'Do you think you could manage to amuse yourself for a bit? I'll be busy for the next half an hour or so. Let's meet at the restaurant – see, there it is – at about one.'

It was easy to amuse herself, Emma found. Slowly she strolled around the camp. It was so different from Skukuza. Smaller, much smaller, more informal, with the bungalows set in half-circles.

She walked down to the fence and looked through the bush and over the river. It was the same river that flowed past Skukuza, that wound along the Lower Sabie Road, down past this camp. Here the view was different, the river not as wide and sweeping and close to the fence as it was at the bigger camp. But it was pretty, so very pretty.

It was nearly lunch-time, and all about her people were returning from their morning drives. Some sat in front of their bungalows, resting and talking, others were beginning to prepare the midday meal. As always there were a few people at the fence, searching the bush with binoculars. A little group stood at one spot, trying to see what a man was pointing to. She sauntered over, and found they were looking at an elephant. But it was far away, only the moving bushes and flapping of a grey ear giving an indication of its presence, and Emma soon moved away, more interested in savouring the atmosphere of the pretty little camp.

The time passed quickly, and before she knew it it was time to join Stewart at the restaurant. 'Hi.' He saw her coming and waved to her. 'It wasn't too boring, I hope?'

'Oh, no, I enjoyed it. It's so different from Skukuza, isn't it?'

'Yes. All the camps have an atmosphere of their own.

61

Lower Sabie is one of my favourites. It's small and pretty. It really does have a lot of charm. Now,' he said, handing her the menu, 'what shall we order?'

It was fun eating their meal under the trees, with shiny blue birds hopping cheekily around the table, always ready to fly on to the table, and to take a bite of food if an unsuspecting diner turned away. 'You should see them at Shingwidzi,' Stewart laughed when Emma commented on them. 'They're a positive nuisance. I took a film once of four of these little chaps busily pecking about in a frying-pan that had the remains of scrambled egg in it.'

'They're cute,' Emma said, smiling. 'And I just love watching the people.'

'Are they cute too?'

'You're teasing me again. They're so interesting, Stewart. Do you know, while I was walking I heard so many different languages spoken . . .'

'And saw so many cameras and tripods.'

'Yes,' she laughed. 'I'm certainly not the only photographer around here. Though,' she added, smiling at him warmly, 'I bet I'm the only one with such a beautiful place to wait at for my pictures. But, Stewart,' she returned to her original thought, 'I came past a little communal fire and there were three men all holding their long forks with meat on the end of them, trying to tell one another what they'd seen. One was Italian, and one was Greek, and one, I think, must have been Scandinavian. Anyway, there they were, trying very hard to make themselves understood, all gabbling in broken English with their own languages thrown in, conversing about the *grandi* li-ons.'

'And understanding one another and getting a tremendous kick out of it all.'

'Oh, yes, they were loving it.'

'Tourists love coming here,' Stewart said. 'Do you

know how the Kruger National Park came to exist at all?'

'No, I don't think I do.'

'The whole country was once swarming with game, thousands upon thousands of miles of bush with wild animals roaming in it. All the big cities – Johannesburg and Cape Town – they were all bush. And if you've ever been to Johannesburg you'd find it hard to imagine that lions once walked down Eloff Street.'

'What happened to the game?' she asked.

'As the cities were built, and as the country became civilized, the game was killed or chased further and further away. Soon there was very little land left with wild animals on it.' He was thoughtful a moment. 'I suppose it's the story of civilization everywhere. When man comes the animals must make room for him. But there was a president, Paul Kruger, one of the early presidents of the Transvaal, and he realized what was happening. He knew that unless something was done soon this country too would have no game left, and so he decided to create an area, a sanctuary, where animals would be free to live their lives without being killed to make way for cities. An area too where no hunters could come to kill for sport. This is the sanctuary, and it was named after him, the Kruger National Park.'

'How wonderful,' Emma said. 'There must be so much that I don't know, that is interesting.'

'There is. Some day you must read a little more about the Park in the early days. You must read about Stevenson Hamilton, one of the most famous of all the game rangers, after whom Skukuza was named.'

'One never realizes how much people really give of themselves. I mean, people must have done so much to create a game sanctuary like this ...' She broke off thoughtfully. 'But it was all worthwhile, wasn't it? I think

63

I can understand how you feel about it, why you love it so much.'

'Can you, Emma?'

'Yes,' she said slowly. 'I'm beginning to understand why this is your life. It's the kind of place that makes you feel this way. Am I right?'

'You are. Could you feel this way about the Park, Emma?'

'I'm – not sure. I haven't been here long enough to tell. But I think I could. This life, the idea of dedicating oneself to the preservation of wild life – I think it begins to grow on one. Yes ... yes, I think I could.' She looked up and found his eyes upon her face, and again there was that look in them that she could not understand, and so found vaguely disturbing.

It was time to go then, and they had a leisurely trip back to Skukuza. When they were nearly at the camp and Emma was thinking that the day could not have been improved upon, Stewart turned to her and said, 'Had any photos developed yet?'

'No, I haven't had a chance.'

'I'm going to Pretoria for a few days – I've got to have talks with people at the Parks Board. Would you like to come with me?'

'Come with you?' She stared at him in surprise.

'It'll all be above-board, if that's what's worrying you.' There was a gentle mocking smile behind his eyes. 'I thought you might like a change. You could do some shopping. And in the evenings we could go out together.'

'Oh, Stewart!' she breathed, wondering if her eyes would betray the happiness she felt. 'I think I'd like that very much.'

CHAPTER FOUR

MORE than once on the trip to Pretoria Emma found herself thinking of Miranda. What did she mean to Stewart? What was her place in his feelings, this beautiful woman who, Lance had said, was Stewart's girl-friend, and was 'mad' about him? Did she know of this trip? Did she know that Stewart had asked Emma to accompany him?

She owed the other girl no loyalty, yet she could not help wondering what she would think if she knew. For Emma had seen the radiance in her face when she talked to him, the expression in her eyes when she smiled. She had seen too the way Stewart leaned towards her, smiling, to catch her words.

It was this last that had made Emma nearly change her mind about going with him. For she knew by now that she must face reality. She was in love with Stewart, in love with this tall lean man who could be at times so mocking and hard, and at other times so gentle and tender.

She was in love with him as she had never been in love before. And it was this that had made her hesitate, had given her reservations. For if Miranda meant something to him, if he loved Miranda, this would be even harder for Emma to accept after the trip than before. Alone in her cottage in the darkness she had spent many hours thinking. And she had come to the conclusion that she would find Stewart in the morning and tell him that she had changed her mind about going with him.

But when she saw him, when the thin brown face smiled down into hers, her decision melted like ice into water. She could no more have told him she was not coming than she could have, in the first instance, prevented herself from falling in love with him. 'I just wanted to know when we were leaving,' she said.

She looked at him now, the gaunt, determined profile, the long-fingered hands that lay relaxed on the wheel, and which, at the same time, showed so much strength in them. He was so different from Jimmy, so different from the man she had once thought she loved. Jimmy, with his ready, easy laughter, and the charm that had made so many women fall for him. Jimmy had been a little like . . . like Lance, it came to her suddenly.

She frowned at the thought. Lance was not at all like Jimmy, really, yet he had seemed quite put out when she had told him where she was going. He had seemed to take it as a personal affront. She had come away from England to get away from complications, and if she were not careful she might find she had landed herself in a new tangle.

Emma sighed.

'That was a heavy sigh.' Stewart looked at her and grinned. 'Not sorry already that you came with me?'

'No.' She was certain the radiance in her eyes must be all too clear. 'Just tired. Not used to all these early mornings.'

As if he had guessed her true thoughts he took his hand from the wheel and squeezed one of hers. 'We're going to have a nice time, Emma. I want you to do just whatever you feel like doing. You needn't consider me at all. In any event I'll be busy most of the day. In the evenings, I thought we could go out together.'

'I don't suppose you have much chance to go out in the Park,' she said.

'Just the odd evening in town. Being able to choose a different entertainment venue three nights in a row will be something special for a country bumpkin like me.'

'I'm looking forward to it,' she said impulsively, deciding at that moment to dismiss Miranda completely from her thoughts. She would live for the moment, taking things just as they came. 'I'm really looking forward to it,' she said again.

'Good.' He smiled at her as he put his hand back on the steering wheel. 'I am too.'

Emma found that though they were going to stay at the same hotel, their rooms were at opposite ends of the passage. 'Satisfied?' Stewart grinned at her mischievously. 'All above-board as I promised you.'

'I wasn't worried. Not one little bit,' she grinned back at him.

While Stewart was at the Parks Board that afternoon, Emma spent the time window-shopping. She found it was pleasant to stroll through the streets of Pretoria, watching the bustle of people, looking in shop windows. It was all so different from England, from London, and from the village she had grown up in. Tomorrow, she would make a few purchases, but today she would just stroll about and look around her.

She was walking past a little boutique when a dress in the window caught her eye. She stared at it for a long time. It was a little more than she normally would have spent, but it was a dress that was made for her, and she knew that in her present mood she could not resist it.

It was a lovely shell pink, a shade that would enhance the soft colouring of her face. A soft, feminine dress, a dress for summer evenings spent with a man she loved. It was a dress she had to own, and at length, deciding she would do without some of the other things she had planned on purchasing, she went into the shop, tried it on, and bought it.

It might be sheer extravagance to have bought a dress

67

like this when she was going to be spending the next three months of her life in the wilds, and the fashions might well have changed after that, but somehow she knew, and she knew it blindly and surely, that this dress was right for her.

Stewart was waiting for her in the foyer of the hotel when she came in, and she saw by the stiffness in his face that he had been worried.

'Where have you been?' His voice was taut.

'Shopping.'

'It's late.'

'Is it? I lost all sense of time. I'm sorry you were worried.'

'I didn't know where you were. You're in a strange town and you don't know the way around. I wouldn't have known where to start looking for you.'

'I'm sorry,' she said again, but in part she was glad, for if this taut, self-sufficient man could be so shaken, did it mean that he cared?

'I made a booking at a restaurant I've been told is pleasant. Just a tentative booking. Evidently the food is good and there's dancing. Would you like to go with me, Emma?'

'I'd love that,' she smiled.

'Well, then, shall we walk for a bit, and then we could both go and get ready.'

The walk did not last long, but it was companionable. There was something strangely exciting about being alone together in a city where nobody knew them. It gave her an impression of isolation, like two people alone together on an island. So different from Skukuza, where in the confines of the camp, big though it was, everyone knew everybody, and private affairs could be bandied about by gossip just as in a village.

When she got back to her room she ran herself a bath

and poured in the crystals she had treated herself to. These too were an extravagance, but this was a day when she wanted to feel feminine and pampered. It was a special day.

She lay in the warm water, thinking of the evening that lay ahead. The thought of dining with him, and dancing ... of drifting around a dance-floor with his arms around her ...

She loved him. She had tried so hard to keep her feelings detached, but she knew now that when you really loved someone it was not a feeling that could be turned on and off at will. Momentarily the thought of Miranda intruded itself. Perhaps the other girl was the one Stewart really liked, perhaps these days together were just an interlude, but be that as it may, Emma knew that she loved him, would always love him, even if he decided to marry the other girl one day.

She got out of the bath, slipped the pink dress over her head, then went to the mirror to put on a little make-up. Her cheeks were flushed from the bath. A few moist tendrils of hair curled over her forehead and her eyes were luminous with excitement. She put on a little lipstick, glad that it matched the dress so well, fluffed a suggestion of blue eye-shadow on to her eyelids, and brushed her hair till it was glossy. Then she walked over to the full-length mirror and spent a few moments inspecting herself.

She knew that she looked her best. The dress was all that she had hoped it would be. It was simple and feminine, with a narrow belt that emphasized the smallness of her waist. She hoped that Stewart would like it too.

He was waiting for her in the lounge when she entered. At first he did not see her. He was sitting at a table, reading a newspaper, and for a few moments Emma stood quite still and watched him. He was wearing a dark grey suit, and it hit her with a tiny shock how distinguished he looked. So accustomed was she to seeing him in a safari suit that she had never thought of him in a lounge suit. With his long lean figure, the tanned face and the thick brown hair, neatly brushed for once, he was the best-looking man in the room.

'Stewart,' she said, at last, softly. 'Stewart . . .'

He looked up and rose quickly to his feet. 'Emma!' He took her hand and his eyes, when he looked down at her, seemed to have deepened in colour. 'Emma, you look . . . you look very beautiful.' His voice was gruff. 'Shall we go?'

It was a magical evening. An evening wrapped in a cocoon of enchantment that nothing could touch. 'I must remember it like this,' she thought once, as they moved together over the dance-floor, his grey-suited arms holding her firmly against him, his chin just touching her hair. 'It can never be quite like this again. I must remember it as it is.'

She knew he felt it too, this special thing that was happening to them. From the moment they had left the lounge together the feeling had been with them, so real that it could almost be touched. It was there in the way he treated her, like some fragile possession that had to be handled lovingly and with great care. It was there in the way they looked at each other over the tops of their wine-glasses. Stewart had leaned towards her, clinked his glass gently against hers, and said, 'To you, Emma. And to . . . to . . . to your happiness.' She had had a feeling for a breathless moment that what he had really meant to say was, 'And to us.' But perhaps, for some reason that she did not know, he was not yet ready to say it.

The feeling had been there when they started to eat. They had ordered a fillet steak each, with mushrooms, and Emma never knew afterwards whether the chef had

had magic hands, for the food was ambrosia, just as the wine had been nectar.

They spoke together, lightly, laughing easily over the same things, serious about the same things too. But when they danced they danced in silence. Stewart made no pretence of holding her stiffly and formally. When they came upon the dance floor he put out his arms to her, and held her close. Now they did not even attempt to speak. His chin touched her hair, and after a few moments she leaned her head against his shoulder and closed her eyes. She wished they could dance like this for ever. If only it had never to end!

When they went back to their table Stewart drew his chair alongside hers, and put his arm around her. They did not talk much now, and the silence between them was not one of strain but that of two people very much in tune with each other, of two people, she hardly dared admit it to herself, in love.

It was late when they came back to the hotel. He took her to the door of the room, and, still holding her hand, he smiled down at her. 'Sleep well, little Emma. I'm going to make an early start tomorrow morning, but you can sleep late. We'll meet again in the evening.'

'Stewart,' she looked up at him tremulously, 'it's been wonderful. Thank you.'

Again there was the deepened colour in his eyes as he looked down at her without speaking. At last he drew her towards him, kissed her once, very gently, and said, 'Thank *you*, Emma.'

When she was alone in her room she looked into her mirror, and she saw what she had known she would see – the face of a woman in love. Even at the height of her happiness with Jimmy she knew she had never looked like this, her cheeks glowing, her eyes soft and with the sparkle of many colours.

This was the face Stewart had seen when he had said, 'Thank *you*, Emma,' and she knew it had betrayed her as nothing else could have.

She could not have said the next morning whether she had slept that night or not. But if she had slept it had been in a half-waking, half-dreaming state, in which she had whirled slowly and continuously round and round a dance-floor, with a grey-suited figure holding her close, smiling down at her with that slow steady smile that made her heart turn over.

The next day she walked the streets of the town in a dream. The shops seemed a fairyland of beautiful things, the people were beautiful, the pavements seemed to float beneath her feet.

In the evening she found Stewart waiting for her. 'Have a good day?' he smiled at her, taking her hand in his. 'What shall we do tonight?' Emma had no suggestions. It was just enough to know that they would be together. 'What about dinner and a show? I see *The Sound of Music* is showing at one of the cinemas. I haven't seen it, country bumpkin that I am, but perhaps you have?'

She had, but did not say so, for she knew that whatever she saw that evening would make little impression on her anyway. It was enough to know that she would be sitting in the darkened cinema, with the man she loved at her side.

In the event, Emma enjoyed the film even more than she had the first time. Stewart took her hand and held it firmly in his, and she let the lovely music and the beautiful scenery wash about her, enjoying every moment of it.

On their third night, their last in Pretoria, they went again to the restaurant they had visited the first evening. Again Emma slipped on the pink dress, and again there was the look on Stewart's face when he saw her. It was a wonderful evening, an evening out of a fantasy world.

When they came at last to their hotel and Stewart stood by the door of her room he looked silently down at her for what seemed a very long moment. It was a moment too precious for words. At last he took her in his arms and said, 'Thank you, Emma. Thank you for coming with me. It's been wonderful.'

She looked at him tremulously, not daring to speak, waiting for him to say the words she longed to hear, and which she sensed he wanted to say. But he only kissed her, then turned abruptly and went back to his own room.

Next morning they made an early start back to the Park. Emma felt a little sad. Soon they would be back at Skukuza, and though she knew she would still see him, she knew too that the little cocoon of enchantment which had enfolded them during these days together would be dissolved.

For in Skukuza Stewart would be plunged once more into his normal routine. Things could not be the way they had been now. If only . . . if only he had said he loved her. He had wanted to, she was certain.

What had kept him back? Was it the thought of Miranda? Involuntarily the girl's face swam before her eyes, in spite of her strict resolve not to think of her. Did he owe her some special loyalty that she did not know of? Or was there another reason altogether?

'So deep in thought.' He was smiling at her.

'Uh-huh.' She smiled back at him.

'Looking forward to going back to camp?'

'I suppose I am,' she said a little wistfully. 'But it *was* lovely, wasn't it?'

'It was.' His voice was gruff as he reached for her hand and held it a moment in his. 'Very lovely.'

Johnny was waiting for her the next morning. 'My dad said I could come with him today, but I thought I'd like to go with you.' He looked at her expectantly, then he added quickly, 'If you want me, that is.'

She laughed. That last bit was not at all typical of the impulsive little youngster, and she knew he was remembering an injunction given him by his parents.

'Of course I want you. I'll be only too delighted to have you with me.'

'All right if I take these?' He produced a sketch pad and pencil from his shorts pockets.

'Fine. I'll take my camera and you'll take your sketch pad and we'll have a right artistic morning.'

'You've never shown me any of your photos,' he said as they were driving slowly away from Skukuza. 'You said you would.'

'I haven't had any to show you till now. But while we were in town I had a few spools developed.'

'You should have brought them with you.'

'I did. When we find somewhere pretty to stop I'll show them to you.'

'Swell!' he grinned.

'Where shall we go today, Johnny?'

'Well . . .' He hesitated.

'Have you anywhere special in mind?' Emma could see that he had.

'There's a hippo-pool. It's very pretty and I thought I'd like to paint it one day. Only thing is . . .'

'Well?' She looked at him curiously.

'Well, there don't seem to be many animals on that road. I don't know whether we'll spot anything much for the camera.'

'I don't mind,' she said easily. 'After all, I'm going to be here quite a long time, and there'll be other times for the camera. In fact,' she turned to him, 'Stewart showed me a

74

beautiful place where I can sit for hours and just watch the animals come down to drink. I believe it's a ranger's road.'

'Stewart showed you that?'

'Yes.'

'He must like you,' observed Johnny.

'Why do you say that, Johnny?'

'Because he wouldn't have taken you there otherwise. That's a special spot — I think I know which it is. He wouldn't let just anyone go there.'

'Oh ...' She hoped he couldn't see the lift his words had given her.

'Of course,' he went on thoughtfully, 'I always knew he liked you.'

'Really, Johnny?'

'Yes. He was disappointed that day you couldn't come with us. When you went with Lance.'

'But ...' She stopped, then couldn't resist the temptation to go on. 'But in the end he had a visitor, so it was just as well, wasn't it?'

'Yes. The Miranda bird,' he said gloomily. 'Oh, hang!'

'What's the matter?'

'She'd like to marry him, I think.'

'Oh!' She would have liked to ask him more, but knew it was not fair to take advantage of the boy's innocence.

'She's always mooning around him. She makes him jam, and she knits him jerseys, did you know?'

'She does?' Emma jerked the car slightly in shock, for she had not realized things were as serious as this.

'Yes. Goofy kind of things to do. That bird's mad about Stewart.'

And Stewart, she wanted to ask, wanted to shout. What about Stewart?

'Emma!' The idea came to him suddenly, and he

turned to her eagerly. 'Why don't you marry him?'

'Oh, Johnny, I can't just . . .'

'No, but, really, you like Stewart, don't you?'

'Yes, I like Stewart,' she agreed.

'And he likes you.' She did not answer so he went on eagerly. 'Go on, Emma, marry him.'

'It's not so simple, Johnny,' she protested.

'Why not?'

'He hasn't asked me.'

'Oh!' The boy was flummoxed. 'Is that all?'

'It's everything.' She gripped the wheel firmly and decided to change the subject. 'Well now, I think I see a fork in the road. Which way do we go now?'

'Left. Look, Emma, I still don't see why you can't . . .'

'Look at that beautiful bird in the trees – there,' she slowed the car to distract him. 'Do you see it?'

'Where? Oh, yes.'

'It's beautiful. I don't think I've ever seen one like it. What is it, Johnny?'

The twelve-year-old boy's interest was quickly diverted. 'It's a hornbill,' he told her. 'Did you know that . . .'

By the time he had finished telling her about the habits of the hornbill he had forgotten the earlier theme, and began to chatter happily about his father's work, school, painting, in fact, anything that happened to pop into his mind.

At last they came to the hippo-pool.

'We can get out here,' Johnny told her. 'It's safe.'

'Are you sure?' asked Emma.

'Of course. Nobody comes to harm here. There's a sign that says you can get out of your car. Look, there.'

'Oh, well, in that case . . .' She glanced nervously about as they walked down the narrow path to the river, expecting at any moment to see a lion pounce from behind a bush. But her fears were forgotten as they came to the rocky outcrop near the edge of the water. 'It's beautiful! Gosh, it really is lovely.'

'It is, isn't it?' His face beamed with pride, almost as if he owned the spot. It really was very beautiful, with the enormous trees framing the vista of deep blue water that curved tantalizingly away from them. In the distance she could see the hippos, almost completely submerged in the water. Emma wondered if she would see them surface, and knew that even if she did not, it would not matter. It was wonderful to sit here in the sun, on the rocks, enjoying the sights and sounds of the river.

'You were going to show me your photos,' Johnny reminded her.

'Yes.' She opened her bag and took out the envelopes.

'Hm.' He looked at them critically, holding them carefully between finger and thumb so that he would not mark them. 'They're not bad. This one of the elephant is good, and I like the one of the monkey family. But this one – the exposure isn't quite right. And this one here, of the kudu, could be sharper. You wouldn't be able to reproduce it like this.'

'You understand quite a lot about photography, don't you?' She looked at him curiously.

'Not all that much. But I want to be an artist, and guess I have to know about all kinds of art.'

Emma smiled at him. She had become very attached to this youngster, so innocent and naïve still, and yet, at times, so very grown up.

'I wish *I* knew a little more,' she said ruefully.

'I'm sure you'll learn,' he reassured her.

'Oh, Johnny,' she leaned towards him and hugged him, 'you're so good for me. I think I will learn. I really want

77

very much to. And now, how about you? Weren't you going to do some sketching?'

He took the sketch pad from his pocket, and was soon absorbed in what he was doing. She watched as his pencil moved over the paper, slowly at first as he got the feel of his subject, and then, as he warmed to what he was doing, his pencil moved more quickly in short sharp movements.

It was a particularly pretty spot, with the trees framing the river scene, and it was the scenery that he was drawing. 'I'll do the animals later,' he told her once, looking up. 'Right now, I'm just preparing the background.' He delved in his pocket and brought out a sticky piece of gum. 'Would you like some?'

She took the piece he offered her, not so much because she wanted it, but because she did not want to break the spirit of camaraderie that existed between them. For a while she watched him, then as he became more and more absorbed in his work, she gave herself up to her own thoughts.

What Johnny had told her about Miranda had upset her more than she cared to admit. It was all very well to convince herself, as she had tried to, that Miranda and Stewart were just friends, that the radiance she had seen in the beautiful face had been imagined. Jam and jerseys could not be imagined away. These were tangible things that could be eaten and worn, and she knew that a woman did not go to the trouble of knitting a jersey for a man unless he meant something in her life.

She remembered Lance's implication that Stewart was playing her up against Miranda to make the other girl jealous. Part of her, the insecure part, wondered if it could be true. If it could have been the reason he had taken her to Pretoria with him.

But in her heart she knew this was not so. She could not

have imagined the look in his eyes when he saw her in the pink dress, imagined the way he held her on the dance-floor. She knew this instinctively, as a woman knows when a man is attracted to her.

And yet . . . She had been so certain he was going to tell her he loved her. She had wondered at the time why he had held back. Did it have something to do with Miranda? Did the other girl mean more to him than he wanted her to know? He liked her, Emma was certain of it, but could it be possible that he was just playing with her?

'Time to go back,' she said at last.

'Ah, shucks.' Johnny was disappointed. 'I still have tons to do.'

'I know, dear, but it's time to have lunch.'

'Can we come again some time?'

'Of course.'

'School's starting soon,' he sighed.

'Oh, Johnny,' she laughed. 'Nobody could say you weren't persistent, could they? We'll come again, I promise.'

They drove back slowly, and though Emma asked Johnny whether he wanted to come with her again in the afternoon, he said he could not. After she had had lunch and a little rest she decided to go to the spot that Stewart had shown her.

It was just as lovely as she remembered it. She sat by the river, concealed from the bank where animals came to drink, and yet with an almost perfect view and camera angle.

It was a perfect afternoon, and she was able to take more pictures than ever before. Happily she clicked, each shot looking just right in her view-finder.

Once she snapped two giraffe who came walking down to the river with their peculiar yet dignified gait. Emma loved to watch them drink. The two back legs straight up and the front legs splaying out to either side, while the long graceful neck curved forward and down. What a beautiful and majestic animal the giraffe was! She thought she would never get tired of watching it.

A herd of impala came to the water, and though she had seen so many of them, each time Emma thought anew how clean and graceful they were, almost as if they had just emerged from a session at a beauty parlour. When the impala had vanished back into the bush, there appeared a group of zebra, shy and strong and very beautiful, together with their friends the wildebeest, who always looked as if they had got out of bed in the morning without combing their hair.

The afternoon was drawing to a close when she saw the leopard. She had not seen it approach, but all of a sudden she became aware of it in a tree. Trembling with excitement, she made her camera ready, waiting for the moment when the leopard would come into the open and she could snap it. It was a rarer animal than the lion, she had discovered, an animal that was seldom seen, for it often hid in trees and hunted by night.

In this lovely setting a picture of a leopard would be a special trophy. Emma lost all concept of time as she waited. Finally, when she was beginning to think it would never move from the fork in the tree, the leopard bounded down, and with exquisite feline grace walked towards the water. Click! She had taken the picture, glad that she had taken the trouble to balance the camera on the edge of the window so that it would not move, and that she had been meticulous about exposure and focusing. Who could know when an opportunity like this would come her way again?

Happily she replaced the camera and the exposure meter in their cases, put the car into gear, and turned off the ranger's road and back on to the main road leading to Skukuza.

Emma was surprised when she came out of the trees to find the setting sun bright in her eyes. It must be later than she had believed. When she glanced at her watch she realized that while she had waited for the leopard to move she had lost all sense of time. It was late afternoon, the sun was bright with the brightness of sunset, and she knew that once it vanished below the horizon it would get dark quickly. She was still some way from the camp and she knew she would have to hurry.

Only a few miles from Skukuza a massive grey shape detached itself from the trees and lumbered into the road in front of her. An elephant. With a shock Emma realized that she had not seen it. In the quickly-darkening landscape it had not been possible to distinguish it from its surroundings. Quickly she slowed to a halt and took out her camera. What a beautiful shot it was! An elephant at such close quarters – it would be a certainty for Sam's book. She was disappointed when she looked at the reading on her exposure meter, and realized it was too dark to take the picture. Then she decided to take a chance, and clicked it anyway.

At length she put the camera away and waited for the elephant to move. But the great beast showed no sign of moving. His trunk was curled about the branch of a tree that leaned outward towards the road, and Emma could hear the snapping of the twigs and the swishing of the leaves as the trunk tightened on the branch.

Impatient now, she edged closer, thinking she might be able to pass the elephant on one side of the road. Seeing what Emma was about to do, the elephant uncurled its trunk, swung it upward, and with a great flapping of ears let out a mighty bellow. Thoroughly frightened now, Emma checked her progress and backed hastily a few yards, keeping the engine running in case the necessity arose to reverse quickly away from a charging elephant.

The elephant glared at her a moment longer, then he swung his trunk back around the branch. It was getting really dark now, and though Emma knew she would have no difficulty finding her way back, she was beginning to feel uneasy. It was a long time since any cars had passed her. What if the elephant should decide to stay in the road all night?

Finally, with a mighty swing of the trunk and another menacing bellow in her direction, the enormous beast lumbered off the road into the bush. With a sigh of relief Emma began to drive forward in the direction of Skukuza.

It was quite dark now, and because the roads were not lit up in the Park at night, the landscape was more than a little eerie. Sometimes a dark shape would loom at the side of the road, standing out perhaps because it was blacker than the surrounding darkness, and Emma would slow down, wondering whether it was an animal, and then, coming alongside it, she would see it was a bush. She was worried that she would bump into an elephant, but then, as her eyes grew accustomed to the darkness, she hoped that she would see an animal long before she could drive into it, and be able to stop.

At last the lights of Skukuza appeared on the horizon, and she knew she could relax. The trip back had had its frightening moments, but nothing drastic had, in the end, happened, and now it was over. She wanted nothing more than to get into the camp, have a bath, something to eat, and then stand at the fence by the river in the evening coolness and let her nerves unwind.

Arriving at Skukuza she found that the gates were locked. Just inside the camp stood a watchman, and around him swarmed an excited group of children, eager to see what was going to happen.

82

'Will you open the gate for me, please?' she called.

No response.

'I want to come in. Could you please open the gate?' A few moments passed before she realized that the gate was not going to be opened before certain formalities, namely the decision regarding a fine, had been completed.

'I was held up,' she tried to explain. 'There was an elephant in the road . . .'

Still no response. She should have been in camp at the time stated on the clock. She was thirty-five minutes late, so she would have to be fined.

It was at this point, while the discussion was still under way, that Emma saw Stewart striding up the gate. 'Stewart!' she called in relief. 'Won't you explain for me?'

'Explain what?' he asked, and his face was unusually stern.

'This lady was late,' said the watchman. 'Thirty-five minutes late. She must be fined before she can come into the camp.'

'It was the elephant. You see . . .' Emma looked unhappily from one stern face to another. Had she really committed such a terrible crime? 'The elephant stood in the road for at least fifteen minutes and I couldn't get past. It would have charged me . . .'

'But you're not fifteen minutes late,' Stewart pointed out, and his voice was quite impersonal, the voice of a stranger. 'What happened to the rest of the time?'

'I was held up.' She was aware of the despair that had crept into her voice. 'I went to the spot you showed me, and saw a leopard, and I wanted to snap it.'

'You disobeyed the rules of the camp for a photograph?' He turned to the man at the gate. 'Let's work out the fine.'

'Well, the lady was thirty-five minutes late . . .'

'Forty minutes by my watch,' Stewart said shortly.

'Shall we make it thirty-five?' said the watchman.

'Forty.' Stewart turned and walked away then without a glance at Emma.

She felt ill by the time the gate of the camp was opened and she was allowed to drive in. It was an accumulation of many things – the trauma of driving in the dark, the shock of finding the gate closed, the crowd that had gathered around, so intensely interested in what was happening. But most of all it was the shock of Stewart's desertion.

Desertion was the way she thought of it. In the moment when she had seen him walk towards her she had thought he was going to smooth matters for her. But he had made them worse, had actually told the man at the gate that she was forty minutes late when he had said she had been thirty-five minutes late.

It was not the fine that had upset her. She had been late, and rules were made to be kept. It was the humiliation, and, most of all, Stewart's cold and silent behaviour.

She could not understand it. There was so much about this tall, strong man that she could not understand. There were times when he could be so tender, when his face and eyes seemed to speak the words that he would not allow his lips to utter. And there were times when he was so autocratic that he could not be reasoned with.

She remembered the first day she had met him, when she had got out of the car to take pictures of the impala. Then, she conceded now, he had had reason to be angry. But today, though she knew she had broken the rules of the camp, she could not help wondering whether a man who felt something more than friendship for a woman would not have bent just a little.

She closed her eyes and tried to remember the evening in Pretoria, when they had danced together in such harmony, when they had been so close. This was her first day back in Skukuza, and already the other evening, those wonderful evenings which she had wished then would never end, seemed a million years ago.

Perhaps she should leave the Park and go back to England. And even as the thought entered her head she dismissed it. For England meant unhappiness and Jimmy. Then came the thought – will Skukuza be unhappiness and Stewart?

Coupled with these thoughts was the awareness of her obligation to Sam, her father's friend. Sam had commissioned her to take photographs for his book. Admittedly, he had asked her to do it because he had known of her need to get away, but the fact remained that she was now under obligation to take the photos. Sam thought she was taking them, was waiting for them, and she could not let him down.

She was standing at a fence by the river, her mind in turmoil, when Lance came up to her.

'You're not looking too happy, little one,' he remarked.

Emma looked up at him. Was it possible that the story had travelled so quickly?

'I'm sorry this had to happen,' he said quietly, reading the question in her eyes. 'But I did warn you about Stewart, didn't I?'

'Was it so terrible?' she whispered. 'Was it?'

'It's a rule of the camp,' he said uncertainly, 'but where you're such friends . . . I know what I would have done in Stewart's case. I'd have seen that the fine was waived.'

'I tried to explain . . . There was an elephant that wouldn't move out of the road. And before that there was a leopard in a tree, and I wanted to take a picture of it. That's how it all started. Knowing leopards are so rare I kept thinking what a wonderful picture it would be and . . . Do *you* understand, Lance?'

'Yes,' he said sympathetically, 'I do. I know what it feels like to want something very much. I know that feeling, Emma.'

She looked at him uncomprehendingly for a moment. There was so much meaning in his words that she knew he was trying to convey something to her, but at this moment she had enough to think about without worrying about anything more.

'And then the time,' she went on, disregarding what Lance was trying to say. 'The man at the gate said thirty-five minutes, but Stewart said forty. He wanted me to get a heavier fine.'

'Hm.' Lance shook his head sympathetically.

'It's not the fact that I had to pay that hurt – it's the rule and that's that. What hurts is that he wanted it this way. I can't understand, Lance. What made him do it?'

'I don't know. Look, Emma, would you like a spot of supper with me? I haven't been able to see much of you lately, my shifts being at such awkward times, and once when I was free you were out with Stewart . . .'

All Emma wanted to do was to crawl into bed, but she said, almost defiantly, as if she was addressing herself to Stewart and not to the man beside her, 'Yes, thank you, Lance, I think I'd like that.'

Lance made a braai for them both and went out of his way to see that the food was tasty and varied, and that she enjoyed herself. Emma did not taste the food she ate, though through her misery she sensed the trouble he had been to and appreciated it.

Afterwards they took a walk through the camp. It was so much like the first evening they had spent together, only then the evening had been filled with novelty and the excitement of new experiences, while now she felt she was weeping a million tears deep within herself, where they could not be seen.

Emma knew with sure and sudden instinct that they would see Stewart, and sure enough, when they had been walking for some time she saw him come in their direction. Emma felt herself freeze. As though he sensed her need Lance took her hand in his, and without a word they went on walking. Stewart came towards them purposefully, unsmiling, and defiantly Emma kept her hand in Lance's. As she had expected, there was no reaction from Stewart. As if she was no more than a casual acquaintance he nodded as he came abreast of them and passed on his way.

It was at that moment that the idea that had been growing in her mind all evening came to a head. Casually she said to Lance, 'I was wondering ... do you think I would be able to get in to one of the other camps for a while?'

He dropped her hand, and when he spoke his voice was mildly sardonic. 'To get away from Stewart?'

'Good gracious, no!' She looked up at him in pretended astonishment. 'Oh, of course I was annoyed at what happened tonight, but Stewart means nothing in my life. I wouldn't let him chase me away from where I want to be.'

'Sure?' He looked at her quizzically.

'Well, of course.' She laughed, and heard the brittle sound of it in her ears. 'We're all adults. Stewart has his own way of doing things. That doesn't concern me. Besides' – she drew a breath – 'there's Miranda, isn't there?'

Lance was silent for a moment, an unreadable expression on his face. 'Yes,' he said quietly, 'there is Miranda.'

'Anyway, to get back to the idea of going to another camp – I want to see a little more of the Park. I haven't been up in the north at all. What do you suggest I do?

Where should I go?'

'There are camps you could go to,' he said slowly. 'Shingwidzi, Letaba, Punda Milia. The question is whether you'd get into them.'

'Oh.'

'They're pretty full at this time of the year. Look,' he took her arm, 'I'll see what I can do for you in the morning.'

'Oh, Lance, thank you!' She smiled up at him gratefully, thinking how handsome he looked standing there in the moonlight, how nice he was, how predictable. She could not imagine him behaving arrogantly. Impulsively she reached up and kissed him lightly on the cheek. 'Thank you, Lance.'

'Thank *you*, dear,' he said gravely. 'I just wish that I could think your kisses could have a little more meaning. But they won't have for me – ever – will they?'

Emma looked at him wordlessly, tears springing to her eyes. 'Come.' He said it gently, sensing all the pent-up unhappiness inside her. 'I'll walk you to your room, and tomorrow I'll let you know whether I've managed to arrange anything for you.'

A hyena laughed near the wall of the camp that night; the shrill maniacal sound nearly drove Emma to frenzy. It was as if it was laughing at her. 'You fool, you utter fool!' it seemed to howl till at last Emma could bear it no longer and buried her head in her pillow to drown out the sound of it.

Suddenly the loneliness and unhappiness overcame her and she began to cry. She cried and cried, for hours it seemed to her, and when she woke up in the morning she found that her pillow was soaked.

CHAPTER FIVE

'You're in luck.' Lance was briskly matter-of-fact in the early morning, his safari suit clean and neatly pressed, his hair curling away from his forehead, and Emma thought how nice he looked.

'Oh, Lance, you've found me something?'

'Shingwidzi. Fancy it?'

'Oh, yes, of course,' she smiled.

'Just one thing,' he added, 'you'll have to share.'

'Oh!' She was a little dismayed, thinking of the way she had given vent to her tears the night before. It was going to be hard to give up her privacy. 'I suppose there's nothing else . . .'

'I'm afraid not. The camps are all completely full, in fact people are being turned away from the gates every day. This . . . well, it just happened. Two girls were sharing a hut in Shingwidzi – they work in the camp. One took ill and had to be taken to hospital. That leaves an empty bed.'

'I see . . .' she said slowly.

'Think about it, Emma. There's no need to take it if you don't want to. You can stay here, you know.'

'No,' she said, suddenly making her decision. 'It's time I spread my wings a little. I'll take it, Lance.'

'In that case I suggest you leave as soon as possible. It's a long drive from here to Shingwidzi. You'll just make it in a day, but you must leave as soon as you can.'

'That's right. I don't want to find myself locked out of the camp.' She smiled ruefully.

'When will you be back? You *will* be back?'

'Yes. I just want to be away from things a little, see

other people, other scenery. You understand, don't you?' she said pleadingly.

'I think so. Good-bye, Emma.' Lance bent and kissed her lightly. 'Have a good time!'

She went down to the fence by the river and stood silently for a few moments looking over the water and into the bush. She was going to miss this view she had grown to love so much. Far in the distance three giraffes were making their way slowly, and in their peculiarly gracious fashion, to the river. Emma would have liked to stop a while and watch them, but remembering Lance's warning she turned and walked to her hut.

It did not take long to pack her possessions, and fortunately it had been agreed that she could have the room back when she wanted it, but she was filled with a sense of desolation when she walked out, carrying her suitcase, and closed the door behind her.

After locking the case in the boot of her car she went to look for Johnny. She could not leave without a few words of farewell to the boy. His face brightened when he saw her, and Emma said, 'Hello there, I was looking for you.'

'Did you think of going to the dam today?' he asked eagerly.

'No, Johnny. I wanted to say good-bye.'

'Good-bye?' he exclaimed incredulously. 'You were going to be here for three months!'

'I'm not leaving the Park,' she explained. 'I'm just going to Shingwidzi.'

'You won't get there and back in a day,' he warned her.

'I'm going to be staying there.'

'Oh.' His face changed, and though he looked disappointed, there was also a slight wariness. 'Is it ... is it because of what happened last night?'

'Of course not,' she said brightly, wondering from whom he had heard the story.

'Are . . . are you sure?'

'I'm sure, Johnny.'

'Will you be coming back?'

'Probably,' she said cautiously.

'When?'

'I don't know. It all depends . . .' She broke off vaguely. Depends on me, on Stewart, on whether I can bear to face him again. On whether I can endure *not* to see him.

'Are you going to say good-bye to Stewart?' Johnny was shifting his feet uncomfortably about in the sand.

'I don't think so, Johnny.'

'But, Emma . . .'

'Stewart had his own reasons for doing what he did last night,' she said at last, 'just as I have my own reasons for going to Shingwidzi. But I don't think it would be a very good idea to go and say good-bye to him.'

'Emma . . .' Johnny began.

'I must go, Johnny,' she said gently. 'Good-bye, my dear. I don't want to be late tonight. I'll see you when I get back. Then we'll go to the hippo-pool again and you can go on with your picture.'

She went then, quickly, without looking back, as much to hide the tears in her eyes as in a resolve not to break down and go back on her decision.

A few minutes later she had turned out of the big gates at Skukuza and was driving along the road that led north. Satara, Letaba, Shingwidzi, Punda Milia – the camps that were situated in the centre and northern part of the Park. The names flowed through her mind, and at another time, in a happier frame of mind, she would have been enchanted with the lovely sound of them. But for the first half hour after leaving Skukuza she was sunk in depression.

The sun climbed higher in the sky. It was a good day for the road, a good day for seeing animals, for already in the short space of time she had been driving she had seen a hyena slink into the bushes, had stopped to watch a roan antelope, that rare and very beautiful species of buck, and had seen families of monkeys and baboons disporting themselves merrily in the trees.

All at once she was impatient with herself. She was being ridiculous. The reasons she had come to Africa had been to escape an unhappy love-affair, and here she was plunging herself into a new one. She would have to be stern with herself. She would enjoy the drive to Shingwidzi, just as she was going to enjoy her stay there. Perhaps she would return to Skukuza, but for the moment she was going to live and enjoy the days as they came, and try not to think about a man who was not for her.

She could not afford to spend too much time with her camera today. If she saw anything really special she would stop for a few minutes, but otherwise she must spend the day driving and make sure that she reached Shingwidzi before sunset.

Emma's frail exterior hid a strength of character that few people would have suspected. Once she made up her mind about something she did her best to carry it through. Now, having decided to push all thoughts of Stewart to the back of her mind, and to concentrate on the scenery all around her, she was beginning to come out from her misery and enjoy herself.

Emma had become deeply interested in the bush, in the vast stretches of veld, the acacias and thorn bushes and long dry grass. The bush had gripped her mind and her emotions, and she could understand how a person, having spent his life in these surroundings, could grow to love it so much that he could never afterwards live in the narrow confines of a city.

The road twisted and turned on its way to the north, and Emma realized that she was beginning to enter a completely new part of the Park, more tropical and very beautiful. She began to see more and more giraffe, and as always she was mesmerized by their lovely majestic grace and dignity.

Once she stopped, forgetting her resolve not to take photos that day, and reached for her camera. Not far from the road, in a clearing, grazed an enormous herd of zebra and wildebeest. Emma had already discovered the strange affinity the two species have for each other. So often where a group of zebra graze, there is a group of wildebeest nearby. She found the wildebeest an amusing creature, with its unkempt, surly appearance, but about the zebra there was a wild and powerful beauty. Stewart had told her about the zebra's shyness, so she stopped the car as quietly as she could to look at them – so like horses with their powerful legs and beautiful bodies, and the lovely black and yellow stripes. She took a few pictures, knowing that it might be some time before she had such an opportunity again, then, putting the car in gear once more, she drove on.

At Satara she stopped. She had heard so much about this little camp that she had a wish to see it. She had not eaten that morning, and now that her spirits had revived hunger seemed to have come too. She decided to eat something at Satara before driving further.

She parked her car under a shady tree and walked about the camp for a while before going to the restaurant. She was delighted by all she saw. With great spreading trees and lawns with flowers, the camp was very appealing. For her, as a headquarters, Skukuza with its many facilities was ideal, but she felt that Satara must be delightful for a few days of rest. After she had walked around for a while she sat down beneath a lovely flowering tree, ordered herself tea and a toasted sandwich, and then, regretfully, returned to her car and drove further.

She came to Letaba, an older camp, and though she would have liked to stop there too she knew she must stay on the road, for it was still some way to Shingwidzi.

On she drove, the scenery becoming ever more tropical, with mopane trees and ilala palms, and exotic birds calling in the trees, and the fallen branches and mounds of dung a testimony to the great herds of elephant that dwelt in this region.

Presently she came to Shingwidzi. She drove to the office and went in to introduce herself.

'Miss Anderson . . .' They had been expecting her and were very friendly. 'Lance from down at Skukuza told us you were coming. Isn't it lucky we had something for you?'

'I believe I'll be sharing?' asked Emma.

'Yes. One of our girls . ad a sudden appendicitis and had to be taken to hospital in the nearest town. Come along, someone will show you to your room.'

A little apprehensively Emma followed the way to her hut. She had been so lucky to have a room to herself at Skukuza, for she knew there were very few single rooms in the Park, and now she found herself wondering whether the girl she was going to share with would resent having her, whether she would be regarded as an intruder.

But all her fears vanished as soon as she saw Rose. The other girl was busy putting away clothing when Emma came into the room.

'Hello.' A lovely smile lit the tanned face. 'You must be Emma. I'm Rose. I work in the office. Golly, that case looks heavy. Let's put it here on the bed, then I'll show you where you can put your things.'

Emma was relieved. She liked the other girl on sight.

There was a twinkle in her eye, and a humorous twist to her mouth that she knew most people must find irresistible.

'I believe your friend is ill . . .' she began.

'Oh, horrors, yes.' The mouth curved whimsically. 'It started the other night. Sandy said she had a tummyache – well, she'd eaten like an absolute glutton. We'd had a braai with some fellows – and I said it served her right for making a pig of herself. Then the pain got worse, and I woke up to find her crying in pain. Well, that's just not like Sandy, and I realized she was really ill. Poor thing, she had quite an acute appendicitis, and it'll be some time before she can come back here.'

'How awful,' sympathized Emma, imagining what an agonizing trip it must have been for the sick girl when she was taken to hospital. 'I hope Sandy won't mind me staying here while she's away?'

'Heavens, no! And I'm delighted to have you. I can't bear to be alone – I'm a chatterbox, my friends tell me. My enemies call me something else, but I won't bother to tell you what because we're going to be friends, aren't we?'

'Of course we are.' Emma found herself laughing. This girl was going to be good for her. It would be hard to remain depressed in her ebullient company.

'Super. You're a photographer, aren't you?'

'How did you know?'

'Lance said so when he phoned from Skukuza. Top priority, he told us, for the girl who's this terrific photographer from England. So top priority it was.'

'Lance was exaggerating,' Emma said, laughing, strangely glad that he had not told the real reason for her wanting to get away. 'It's true that I'm here to take photos, but I'm not any kind of terrific photographer.'

'What are the photos for?' asked Rose.

'For a book. A friend in England is writing a book about his experiences here in the Park, and I'm doing the pictures.'

'Ah! Perhaps Lance had a point after all. Finished, Emma? Oh, that gown, fling it up there on the hook with mine. I'm off duty right now. Come along, I'll introduce you to the others.'

It was fairly late in the afternoon by the time Emma had unpacked her things, had had a shower and been introduced by Rose to several of the young people in the camp. Now it was dark, and she sat by a fire, eating a piece of *boerewors*, and letting the sensations of this different camp wash over her.

All her fears that she would be alone and miserable had been dispelled, first when she had met Rose, and then, a little later, when she had been introduced to a group of young people who were spending a few days in the Park, and who had invited the two girls to have a braai with them.

The supper was fun. The young men stood about the fire, holding meat at the end of long pronged sticks, and there were jokes and laughter and anecdotes in abundance.

By the time they had finished their meal a feeling of contentment pervaded them all. Overhead a million stars blazed in the African sky, all around them was the incessant sound of the crickets, and from further off came the muted sounds of talk and laughter from other fires.

One young man produced a guitar and began to strum it softly. At first the tunes he played were soft and sad, and for some reason they brought tears to Emma's eyes, so that she was glad it was too dark for the others to see.

But after a while his mood began to change. The music became quicker and livelier, and the young people began to clap in time to its beat, and then, as the tunes became the ones they knew, they sang. Some of the songs were strange to Emma, and she sat quietly listening to the words of the traditional folk tunes, enjoying the rhythm and the unison of voices. Then the guitar swung into songs she knew, and she joined in the singing.

After a while it began to grow chilly. During the day it had been hot, as the sun beat down fiercely, but at night it could grow very cold. A glowing heap of embers was all that remained of the fire, and Emma moved nearer to their warmth. But presently even the last glow was gone.

It was quiet now in the camp. Children had long since gone to bed, grown-ups had finished their beers, and their chats, and were beginning to turn in for the night. In the Park, where people tended to rise well before sunrise, they went to bed early.

It was time for the little group about the burnt-out fire to break up and go to their huts. It had been a pleasant evening, and Emma was surprised to find how much she had enjoyed herself. 'Well, folks, see you all tomorrow.' The bearded guitar-player lifted his instrument, and there was a chorus of good nights. Then Emma went with Rose to the little hut.

It had been a long day, an emotional day, a day of almost continuous driving. While she had sat by the fire Emma had been unaware of her tiredness, but when she lay down at last and pulled the blankets over her, the fatigue hit her. She was so tired that she could not feel emotion, and though for a few moments before she fell asleep the face of a tall tanned figure hovered before her eyes, she was too tired to feel sadness, and within minutes she was asleep.

When she awoke next morning Rose had already left the hut and she was alone. Emma was surprised to find that the sun was already fairly high in the sky, and when she pushed aside the curtains and peered out of the window she saw that many cars had left for the day. She must have been really tired.

Now, however, after so many hours of deep sleep she felt fresh and eager to face the day. Quickly she washed and dressed, then left the room to see what she could do about breakfast. Today she would take things easy, and not worry about getting out early to take photographs.

The invigorating feeling she had woken up with seemed to have affected even her appetite, and in spite of the delicious braai the night before, she found she was hungry. She made herself two eggs and bacon and a cup of hot coffee, all of which she consumed with great relish. Then, breakfast over, she strolled around the camp.

She had arrived so late on the previous day, and had been so eager to get settled, that she had taken little note of the camp itself, and now she was enchanted with all she saw. Shingwidzi was completely different from the other camps she had seen and, perhaps even more than the others, with a character and charm all its own.

The whole atmosphere of the camp was tropical. Big beautiful trees grew everywhere, mopani and ilala palms and lovely exotic shrubs were in profusion. The little birds she had seen at Lower Sabie were here in great numbers, pecking busily at scraps on the ground, darting hither and thither, blue and mischievous and appealing. It was a ruggedly beautiful camp, and one which Emma knew she could grow to love.

When at last she decided to go for a drive, and turned northwards in the direction of Punda Milia and Pafuri, this last place being the northernmost spot in the Park, she saw how very different the scenery was from all she had seen heretofore.

She was now travelling in the topmost section of the

Park, and the rolling grasslands, with the acacias and profusion of thorny bush, had given way to a much more tropical landscape. Here everything was lush and dense and very green.

On each side of the road was the jungle, thick and green and impenetrable. Emma doubted if it was possible to see any game unless it was on the road. The road went up and down, winding this way and that, so that she had to drive very carefully, not only to avoid hitting an oncoming car, but also because she was never certain whether she might not bump into an elephant at the top of a rise or on the turn of a bend.

For this was elephant country. Great herds of the big beasts lived in this part of the Park, and the many piles of dung on the road bore testimony to their presence.

She was fascinated by the beautiful and unusual trees all about her – knobthorns and wild-date palms, the leadwood, the marula and the fever tree. She identified them all from the book she had bought on the day of her meeting with Johnny.

Now, on the road that led to Pafuri, she came across the most exciting tree of all, an enormous tree, with a gargantuan trunk, and topped by many-twigged branches, a tree which looked as if it had been born when the world began. Emma could imagine prehistoric creatures making their homes in its trunk just as if it had been a cave.

She flipped the pages of her book until she came to it. A baobab! Stewart had told her about this tree, had said he hoped to take her north one day to see it. At the time she had wondered what made this tree so special. Now she knew. For a long time she sat and gazed at it. The unbelievable girth of it, its curious dignity and prehistoric appearance. The drive to Pafuri would have been worth while if only for the chance to see this tree.

Emma soon grew accustomed to life in the beautiful northern camp, and found she was happy there. She became very fond of Rose, her room-mate, her days were filled with activity, and the evenings by the camp-fire, with guitar-playing and singing, were fun.

Only at night did she lie and think of Stewart. She wondered how long it would take her to get over him. Would she ever manage to forget him? Often, against her will, she would be back on the dance-floor with him, back in the lovely cocoon of enchantment. And then her mind would jerk again to reality and she would wonder once more why Stewart had wanted her to be punished. She had broken a camp rule, this she knew. She knew too that it was right that she should have had to pay for it. But what she could not understand was why Stewart had gone out of his way to magnify her crime.

CHAPTER SIX

Time passed, happy carefree days merging one into another, and Emma was astonished one morning to realize that she had been nearly two weeks in Shingwidzi.

It was a burning hot day. Overhead the clouds were heavy, and the oppressive sultriness had decided her to return to camp early. She went to her room, put away the cameras, then went to the restaurant for a cup of tea and something to eat.

She sipped her tea slowly, eating the sandwich without really tasting it. The little blue birds hopped busily about, waiting for an unsuspecting human to look away from the table, but for once their cheeky antics failed to amuse her. She wondered whether it was only the sultriness that accounted for her feeling of apathy.

Listlessly Emma wondered what she should do that afternoon. During the last few days she had travelled the roads that led from Shingwidzi north to Pafuri, and Punda Milia and Babalala, and she had taken the circular road past Tsange Hill with its lovely view, and the pretty Shawo River Road to the south. But, today, none of these drives appealed to her.

She was missing Skukuza – she had known it now for several days. She was missing Skukuza, not only because of Stewart – and she was missing him more than she had feared she would – but, also, she missed it because it was the ideal camp for a headquarters.

Early in her stay at Skukuza she had discovered the camp library, and with her growing interest in the Park and its animals had begun to make good use of its books. Emma had become more and more fascinated with the bush. Far from growing accustomed to its mystery and vastness, she began to find it more and more alluring. She was growing to love the animals, getting to know their habits and the way they lived, and she began to understand more and more why Stewart had chosen this to be his life.

Slowly she sipped her tea, and then, finding she was still thirsty, began to pour herself another cup.

'Any left for me?' For a long moment she did not trust herself to look up. The low deep tone had in it the tender teasing quality which she heard in her dreams every night. Could she be dreaming now? Very carefully she replaced the pot on the tray.

'Well, what about it?' came the voice again. 'Do you think there might be some left?'

Slowly, forcing herself not to tremble, Emma looked up. 'Stewart . . .?' She said it hesitantly, not trusting her voice too far.

'It's me. Did you think I was a ghost?' The words were light, but the eyes held the expression she remembered from the evening when he had held his arms around her on the dance-floor.

'What . . . I don't understand.'

'You still haven't answered my question.' He sat down.

'Question?' she repeated stupidly. 'Oh, the tea . . . Oh, yes, Stewart, I'm sure there's some left.'

'I'm glad. I was beginning to get worried.'

'But what . . . I don't understand . . . why are you here?' she stammered.

'Johnny and I have been discussing things. We decided it was about time that you came home.'

'Oh, Stewart!' The word home had brought such a lump to her throat that she could not speak.

'Well, Emma,' he said gently. 'Will you come?'

She looked at him wordlessly.

'Will you, Emma?' he repeated.

'Yes! Yes, I'll come.'

'Good.' He smiled at her, that rare slow smile that made her heart turn over, and she saw that he was pleased.

'When will we go, Stewart?' she asked.

'In a day or two. I have a little business here. Anyone could come for that, but I decided I wanted to be the one to come. So it'll be another day or so.'

'I'm glad. I couldn't just have left.'

'So you really have enjoyed staying here?' He looked at her curiously.

'Yes. It's a beautiful camp, isn't it?'

'Very.'

'I've been sharing a room with Rose. Do you know her? She's been so nice to me. Made me feel so at home, when she really didn't have to.'

'Rose is a nice lass,' he agreed.

'And then there are a few chaps. We've had braais together, and we've spent the evenings singing round the camp-fire.'

'Sure you really want to go?' he said teasingly.

'Quite sure,' she said softly, knowing that all she felt was there in her eyes for him to read.

When Rose heard she was going she was not surprised. 'So it's Stewart,' she said thoughtfully.

'Did it have to be somebody?' Emma queried.

'Yes. Yes, I think so. When you first came here there was a look in your eyes . . . as if you'd been hurt. You looked bewildered and unhappy, and I thought to myself, Rose, old girl, there's a man in this somewhere.'

'Was it so obvious, then?' asked Emma ruefully.

'Pretty obvious,' Rose said gently. 'Stewart's a good man, Emma. He's hard and tough, and he can be very unpredictable. But he's good. I hope things work out for you.'

'Thanks,' Emma said unsteadily. 'Thank you for everything.'

The drive back south was wonderful, and Emma was content to sit quietly next to Stewart, glancing now and then at the stern profile, at the strong muscled hands on the wheel. She really felt as if she were going back home, back where she belonged.

And yet, she knew, it was not as simple as Rose had seemed to think. She knew that she loved Stewart. That fact, at least, was simple and clear and uncomplicated. But what about Stewart? What did he feel? When he looked at her with the tender expression in his eyes, at those times she thought that he loved her too. But if so, why was he so unpredictable? Why the scene at the gate? Who was Miranda, and what did she mean to him?

No, things were far from simple, but for the moment it was enough to be beside him once more, to be able to look at him, to know that she was going back.

'Have you forgiven me for that evening?' he asked once, very quietly.

'If I could understand why you did it,' she said uncertainly.

He did not answer, only looked at her steadily with an unfathomable expression in his eyes. After a moment he spoke of something else and did not mention the subject again. And Emma realized that things were far from simple.

They spent the night at Satara where Emma was able to share a room with two other girls. She felt the night belonged to her as she sat with Stewart later at a glowing fire, and ate their braai. Sometimes in the past, with camp life, she had had the feeling as if all the fires were merged into one, that all the people were linked by a special bond, a sense of belonging, of shared experiences. But tonight she felt that their tiny fire was an island, a small glowing haven in the midst of all the darkness. When they had eaten they walked slowly round the camp together. Once she tripped on a stone and almost fell, but Stewart seized her arm and kept her steady. And when they walked on he slid his hand down her arm to her wrist, took her hand, and kept it in his.

All too soon the evening ended. That night Emma lay sleepless for a long time, listening to the sounds of the bush beyond the fence, and she knew that she was happy. For she was, indeed, going home.

Next day they came to Skukuza, and it was really just like a homecoming.

'See you a little later,' said Stewart, dropping her at her room. 'I'll give you half an hour, then I'll meet you on the verandah for tea.'

'Lovely!' With a singing heart Emma opened the door of her room and stopped still as she looked inside. On the little table beside her bed was a plant in a pot, an exotic white flower with a heady scent. And beside the pot was a watercolour, a klipspringer in a shady glade.

'Johnny!' she exclaimed joyfully. The gifts were simple but heartfelt, and she felt as if her heart would burst with happiness. So it was true that she had been missed, and that they were glad to have her back.

Quickly she unpacked, had a shower, then went in the direction of the restaurant. Glancing at her watch, she saw she had a few minutes to spare before meeting Stewart, and she decided to say hello to Lance.

'So you're back.' His tone was so sardonic that the smile froze upon her lips.

'Aren't you glad to see me?' she asked, in surprise.

'Very.'

'Then I don't understand, Lance.'

'I was just thinking how hunky-dory it all is. Stewart frowns and you run away. He smiles and beckons a finger, 'and you run back.'

'It's not like that at all,' she burst out, shocked.

'Isn't it?' Lance drawled, and for a moment she felt herself dislike him.

'Of course not. My going had nothing to do with Stewart.'

'Pardon me, Emma, I thought it had.'

'Lance, you're being horrid! I've come here for three months to take pictures – you know that. It would have been madness to spend all that time at Skukuza. I thought I'd explained that.'

'You did,' he said coldly.

'Then what are you trying to suggest? What are you so angry about?'

'I'm not angry, just curious. Just curious to know how you feel about our efficient game ranger.'

'He's a friend, Lance,' she said steadily. 'Just as you are my friend.'

'And would you have come back so readily if I'd been the one to fetch you?'

'I came back,' she said quietly, 'because it was time to come back. Nothing personal, Lance. Please, don't make an issue of this. I was so happy to come back . . .'

'And now I've made you angry.' He was immediately contrite. He smiled then, showing the flash of even white teeth. 'I'm sorry, Emma. I guess I'm a little jealous of Stewart, and just now I couldn't help showing it.'

'You're jealous of Stewart?' she asked wonderingly.

'You like him very much, don't you?'

'I like you both,' she said, non-committally.

He seemed about to say something, then thought better of it. 'Well, that's fine, then, sweetheart,' he said at last. 'Because I like *you*. I like you very much, and I hope you'll remember it.'

Emma felt a little depressed as she walked on. The

lovely light feeling had vanished, and she wondered whether she was letting herself in for a new round of complications. At least at Shingwidzi there had been no emotional demands made upon her. She hoped it was not all going to start again.

Emma stopped for a moment when she came to the broad verandah, scanning the tables for a familiar face. Then she saw him, the muscled brown arm raised in greeting, and with a lifting of the heart she walked quickly up to them. They stood as she came towards them, Stewart and Johnny, the two people she had grown so fond of, and at the same moment they smiled.

'Johnny!' She put her arm around him and kissed his cheek. 'Oh, Johnny, it's so wonderful to see you!'

'Do I get a kiss too?' Stewart grinned.

She coloured as she laughed up at him, then sat down on the chair he pulled out for her. 'Oh, Johnny, thank you for the lovely presents.'

'Only one present is from me,' the boy said, beaming.

'The watercolour. You did that, I know. But the plant, Johnny, wasn't that from you?'

'No.' The smile grew wider.

'Then . . .' Emma looked questioningly from one smiling face to the other. 'Stewart, was it . . . is it . . . was the plant from you?'

'It was.'

'Oh, Stewart!' She was overwhelmed and more moved by the little gift than she had been for as long as she could remember. For it meant he had taken the trouble to make her welcome. 'Oh, Stewart, thank you.'

'I'm glad you like it,' he said a little gruffly. 'Well, folks, I don't know about you, but I'm thirsty. It's been a long trip. What shall we have?'

They sat sipping cool drinks, in perfect harmony with each other. Afterwards they walked down to the river, and Emma leaned her arms on the fence and stared into the bush. The river was broad and green and tranquil, just as she had remembered it. Beyond it stretched the bushveld, a vast and glorious vista in all shades of grey and green and brown, deceptively peaceful beneath the setting sun. Emma stared into the bush, searching for game, but though she could see nothing she knew animals were there, feeding, giving birth, hunting and being hunted.

'It's good to be back,' she sighed happily, turning to the males on either side of her.

'It's super to have you back,' said Johnny, his face glowing, and Stewart, though he said nothing, smiled at her, and after a moment she smiled back.

'Like to come out with me again, Johnny?' Emma asked.

'Oh, yes. I'd like to go on with the painting I started at the hippo-pool.'

'Of course . . .' Emma began.

'Now, Johnny!' Stewart was laughing as he interrupted. 'Emma's hardly back and you're filling up her time.'

'But I'd like to go there with Johnny. I suppose you'll be going back to school soon?' she asked him.

'Yes. There's going to be a competition in town, an art competition. Mom read about it in the paper . . . And boys my age are allowed to enter. I'd just love to have a go with the picture of the hippo-pool.'

'And so you shall,' Emma promised him. 'I'd be so proud if you won.'

'This is one of our worst headaches,' Stewart said as they drove over a bridge. He stopped the jeep and gestured. Below them ran the course of a river, but it was dry, the river-bed sun-baked and hard, the sand corroded and marked with the imprints of many hooves. 'This is one of our tragedies.'

'What happens to the water?' Emma had crossed many such rivers, but had never before given the matter much thought.

'Drought. Once the summer rains fall there may be water here. Again, there may not. But one can't be certain ...' He made a gesture of futility. 'We've been plagued by drought for too long now. Some parts of the Park don't get rain for years at a time, and this' – he gestured again – 'is the result. Do you know what they say about a river like this?'

She shook her head.

'There's a saying that if a man falls into these rivers his feet get dusty.'

Emma smiled.

'Yes, that's a joke. But the reality is not at all funny. Perhaps you can imagine the plight of thousands of animals who come to the river, frantic for water, and find only dry sand.'

'And yet there *are* rivers, aren't there?' Emma asked, thinking of the broad stretch of water that flowed past Skukuza.

'Yes, there are. But the problem is to get the animals to the areas where the water is.'

'I'd have thought they would just go there,' remarked Emma.

'It's not as simple as that. Animals are creatures of habit. They become accustomed to drinking at the same spot every day, and when that dam or river dries up they'll dig holes in the sand in an attempt to find a few drops of moisture.'

'And do they find it?'

'Sometimes. Often there *is* a tiny reservoir of water beneath the sand. But that soon dries up too, and then the position becomes desperate. Also,' he was thoughtful a moment, 'it depends on the type of game. Buck can get by on just a little water. Elephants, as you can imagine, need gallons each time they drink. A few drops beneath the sand is just not sufficient for them.'

'Is there anything you can do?' Emma asked.

'We sink bore-holes, and we erect great concrete troughs of water. But those dry up too. Then we have to find new supplies.'

'I'd never realized all this,' she said wonderingly.

'The problem is to get the animals away from the drought-stricken areas and to the places where the water is. That's one of our most important tasks as game rangers.'

Emma was silent as they drove further. There was so much she did not know, so much she must learn. *Must* learn? Wanted to learn, she thought in wonder.

When she had first come to the Park, she had not been aware there were such men as game rangers, and then when she had met Stewart she still had not known what a game ranger's work entailed. Slowly she was learning. Stewart had begun to take her with him more and more often now, and her interest and fascination in animals, in the bush, in the way of life of the people who worked here, had grown ever greater.

She looked at the lean muscled body beside her and felt a moment of pride. This was a man, a man who was doing a man's work. And this, she knew with sudden certainty, was important to her.

She had learnt of the game rangers' dedication to animals. This enormous Park was a sanctuary to protect the wild life from people, from encroaching civilization that destroyed all nature in its wake, from hunters who killed senselessly and for sport. But the protection did not end at this point. For sometimes, Emma was to learn, the animals had also to be protected against some of the forces of nature which acted against them.

'Why don't you stop lions from killing buck?' Emma asked once, then realizing she was being naïve, said, 'That was a stupid question, wasn't it?'

'Not stupid at all,' said Stewart. 'But obviously it's something we couldn't do. This isn't a zoo – I think I told you that once' – he smiled at her – 'very early in our acquaintance. Lions need meat. Not only lions, but all the predators, the leopards and cheetahs and hyenas. And we can't throw them meat as if they were in cages.'

'You couldn't find a way?' she ventured.

'No. It's the law of nature, the law of the jungle, and it's something you can't interfere with. Besides, predators are not all evil, you know. And they do serve a purpose.'

'They do?'

'If the buck were allowed to breed without any interference they would become a nuisance, and would have to be thinned out. Over-population brings its own problems. But there *are* times when we interfere. If an animal mother is killed and the baby is left defenceless, then we step in and try to rescue it. A baby buck or zebra, any animal really, is so helpless without its mother. It hasn't yet learnt the laws of the jungle and needs to be protected, otherwise it wouldn't stand a chance of survival.'

The road curved back to the dry river-bed and they saw a small herd of impala standing listlessly by a clump of sun-scorched acacias. 'Look.' Stewart stopped the car. On the dry banks of the river two of the herd were making frantic movements with their hooves.

'What are they doing?' Emma asked.

'Looking for water. They may find a little – I don't know. This river has been dry a long time. But things are even worse where a dam or water-hole has just recently dried out, for when the water dries up mud is left, slimy mud-holes that are terribly treacherous. The animals come to these holes because there was water there once, and then they get stuck in the mud. Once that happens they're easy prey for the predators, the lions and the hyenas and the cheetahs. There's no chase then, no hunt. The predators wait for the animals to get stuck in the mud and pick them off.'

'How horrible!' whispered Emma.

'Yes,' Stewart agreed, 'it *is* horrible. And this is where we come in. First of all, we watch for drying-up water-holes so that we can sink new bore-holes, and we try to move the game around. Then, when animals are thirst-crazed and get stuck in the mud, in full view of the lions, we help out there too.'

'I hadn't realized . . . I'd never dreamt . . .'

'Emma,' Stewart said slowly, 'would you like to see a little of what I'm talking about?'

'Oh, yes.'

'It's not a pretty sight, my dear. You'll feel sickened. But it's something you should see if you really want to understand more about the Park and the game.'

And about the game rangers, she thought silently. It filled her with a deep sense of contentment that this man should want her to see more of the life he led. She sensed that what he would show her was something tourists seldom saw, but the fact that he was prepared to take her there showed that he was gaining confidence in her, was beginning to take her seriously, as a person in her own right. And she knew in her heart how very much this meant to her.

It was a dam that he took her to, a dam that had once been filled with water, he told her. Animals had come to this place to drink, had sauntered slowly down through the bush and the scrub and the trees, grazing as they went, each coming to the water in its own time. This had been a beautiful spot once, and the animals had come in great numbers to drink from it.

But it was beautiful no longer. Emma had to stifle the sense of nausea that threatened to overcome her as she gazed down upon the macabre scene. The dam had dried up. For a few years now no rain had fallen, the water that had remained in the dam had been exhausted by the thousands of animals who came to drink from its banks, and what was left had been evaporated by the hot African sun. Now there was no more water, but where the water had been there was mud, slimy, slithery, clinging, teacherous mud.

All around the dam were animals. Thirst-crazed, they stumbled along, dragging their feet from the clinging mud only to become bogged down again at the next step.

And then there were the predators, silent and watching. Emma counted seven lions and three cheetahs. 'Won't they attack?' she whispered in horror.

'If they're hungry. They've probably eaten so much they can't move by now.'

'But the animals . . . Don't they see them?'

'They see them, but they don't care. All they care about is finding water.'

Emma watched as a zebra, its eyes glazed and dull, plodded through the bush, past the car, then down towards the dam and into the mud. It was pitiful to see the slow dragging passage through the sludge. The beautiful animal stopped once, and, shaking its hooves free as best as it could from the sludge that enveloped them, tried to dig into the mud to find water. At last it began to move again.

And then, when it was nearly off the mud, the lions attacked. There was no thrill to the kill, no triumph of the hunter over the hunted, no sense of having outwitted an animal aware of its danger. The lions just pounced on the phlegmatic animal and in a few moments it was all over.

It was like a scene out of a nightmare – the dying animals, maddened and made senseless by their longing for water. The predators, thirsty too, and sated by their easy conquests, sitting on the edge of the dam watching. The herds of apathetic animals that entrapped themselves in that terrible mud for the water they had been accustomed to drink there. Overhead wheeled the vultures, those ugly birds of prey, who always seemed to Emma to smell of death. Wherever a kill was made the vultures were nearby, hovering in the air, ready for their pickings at the time when the lions had finished their meal.

The only bit of hope and sanity in the scene that was so macabre was the sight of the game rangers. Tirelessly they worked, rescuing animals that were weak or young and could not manage to struggle free from the terrible mud.

Asking if Emma would be all right by herself, Stewart went to join them. For a long time she watched them, this dedicated band of men, working together to save the animals from their dreadful fate. The sun was burning down upon them, and the mud dragged at their heels, but still they worked, bringing animals out of the mud, feeding baby animals with sips from baby bottles, pulling out the weak and old that could no longer extract themselves without help.

Once she saw Stewart wipe the sweat from his face, shake his head as though in anger or in despair at something one of the other men said to him, then go back into the mud to work some more.

She watched as he rescued a tiny impala. With infinite tenderness he handled the small animal, and her heart went out to him. The whole scene was a nightmare, but it gave her an insight into this man that she would never otherwise have had.

She saw him come towards the car holding the tiny impala in his arms, and then, as he opened the door, she saw that he held a bottle with a teat in one hand. 'Think you can feed this little mite?' he asked.

'Oh, yes,' she said tremulously, and then, detaining him, as he began to move away again, 'Stewart, will you be all right? All those lions . . .'

'We'll be all right. We've got guns, but we shan't need them.' He smiled at her a moment, weariness and despair in his eyes. 'Feed this baby for me. That will be your contribution.'

He leaned forward, kissed her lightly, and was gone. Awkwardly Emma manoeuvred the little animal in her arms. It was quite unlike anything she had ever held before, not like a kitten or a puppy that fitted into the contours of her body without any trouble.

It seemed all long legs, this little wild thing, and for a few moments it struggled against her, frightened and anxious, trying to get away. Then, as if it realized she was a friend, it began to calm and snuggled against her. The enormous liquid black eyes looked up at her trustfully and it made tiny mewing noises as she brought the bottle to its mouth.

Emma felt an immense surge of tenderness as she held the tiny wild creature in her arms, and watched it drink from a baby's bottle. 'You're a little Bambi,' she said softly. 'A lovely little Bambi. My mother used to read to me about you when I was small.'

How amazed her mother would be to see her now, all alone in a jeep, with the hot African sun blazing down on her, with lions and cheetahs and all manner of other wild animals within yards of her, while she nursed a little wild buck in her arms.

This is as far away from England as I'll ever be, she thought ruefully, remembering her parents' cottage with its climbing roses and its hollyhocks, the daffodils and the primroses, with all the gentle and appealing beauty that was England.

When her parents had consented to her coming here they never could have imagined the savagery, the earthiness and the sheer excitement that she was now a part of. Much as the scene before her sickened her, she knew too that she loved it here, loved the life, the dedication to nature and the creatures of the wild, the magic and the beauty, the harshness that was the essence of life and death.

After a while Stewart came to her and took away the little impala, and brought another in its place, another tiny creature of the wilds for whom, all at once, life had become too much to cope with. And after she had fed this little animal, he brought a young kudu, and then a small zebra. Emma fed them all, nursed them, wondering at herself, at the thought that the girl from England was feeding desperate animals in the African bush.

And so the day wore on. The sun burned down with ever-fiercer intensity, more and more animals stumbled through the sludge and made desperate digging movements in their craving for water. Above the vultures soared and waited, while the sated predators on the edge of the dam slept and waited and watched.

Once Stewart came to the car, and, after wiping his moist dusty face with a handkerchief, he took out a thermos and some sandwiches. 'Not fair to make you suffer along with the rest of us,' he said, as he waited for her to pour him some coffee.

'I'm not suffering,' she told him. 'I'm just sitting here.'

'But it's hot, terribly hot. And you're not used to it as we are.'

'I'd hardly noticed it,' she said, surprised to find this was true. 'I just wish I could do more to help.'

'You *are* helping.' His smile was gentle. 'By helping to feed these little ones you're releasing one more ranger from this duty, and allowing him to help pull the animals from the mud.'

'Oh.' She was absurdly glad.

'Sorry you came?'

'No. No, Stewart, I'm not.' She paused a moment, wondering how she could explain her feelings. 'Obviously, I'm not actually enjoying this – I'd have to be perverted in some way to enjoy the sight of all this suffering. But I'm glad I'm here. I . . . It gives me a feeling of belonging to something, to something that's worth while.'

His eyes deepened as he looked at her, and for a breathless moment Emma wondered what he was going to say. But he only smiled, leaned forward and wiped his handkerchief along her own moist brow, and said, 'I'm glad you feel this way, Emma.' Then he stretched his arms and sighed. 'Well, back to work.'

The hours passed. The fierceness of the sun began to lessen. More and more weak animals had been brought to safety. Presently it was time to go. 'It's not safe to drive after dark,' Stewart told her when he came at last to the jeep and they set off back to Skukuza.

'You must be tired,' she said softly.

'I am,' he agreed wearily.

'I never dreamed that you do work like this,' she said shyly.

'You no doubt thought I spent all my time sitting at Skukuza sipping cool drinks.' He grinned wryly. 'Disappointed, Emma? This is hardly a glamour job, is it? I don't come home after work in a white collar, with a newspaper in my hand. It must seem rough work to you after what you're used to.'

'It's a man's job,' she said simply.

'That it is.' He looked at her for a moment with one of those unfathomable expressions in his eyes. 'That it is.'

Stewart looked so tired, so unutterably weary, that Emma left him in peace, so that he could drive without the strain of having to make conversation. The silence between them was companionable, the silence of two people who have shared an experience, who are thinking the same thoughts, who do not need words to communicate.

As they drove through the deepening shadows Emma thought, 'I'm happy. It's been a hard day, unexpected and cruel and with no punches spared.' But it had something earthy and basic about it that she had found exhilarating. There had been the sense of helping animals that had been extremely satisfying. It had been a day, she knew, that she would remember for a long time to come.

CHAPTER SEVEN

AFTER the day she had spent with Stewart at the dam, the drying-up dam where the game rangers had worked so tirelessly, and she, in her own small way, had lent a hand, Emma's days seemed to acquire a new dimension. Stewart began to take her about with him more and more. He showed her sights she knew no ordinary tourist would have seen. He spoke to her about his work, about his dreams for the Park and for the animals, and about the many things he would like to see put into operation if finance and practicality were not factors involved.

More and more he spoke to her about himself – not about his life before he came to the Park, about his life with Mary, but about the ambitions and dreams that pertained to his work.

It was as if, having accepted her as a real person, and not just as a visitor come to while away a few months before going back to civilization, he had come to enjoy her company. It seemed to Emma sometimes that Stewart was essentially a lonely man, that all these things he now told her had been bottled up inside him for too long. It was as if he was beginning to see her almost as a dimension of himself.

But even while she cherished their time together she wished that he would say something that would give her hope that they might have a future together. Slowly, inexorably, the time was passing, and when the three months were up she would have to pack her case, take up her cameras, look her last at the little hut which had become for this short period home, and then she would go back to England.

She knew by now how much she wanted to stay – stay for ever in Africa, in this animal sanctuary, in the bush-veld, with the man she loved.

Thus far, however, he had given her no indication of his own feelings, had never by a spoken word said that he would like her to stay. The expression she caught sometimes in his eyes, the moments of tenderness and understanding, these were not enough. If he wanted her to stay he would have to say so, and so far there had been no sign that he intended to.

At her low moments Emma would wonder whether what she took to be deeper feelings were nothing more, on his part, than the enjoyment of congenial company, the satisfaction of talking to somebody who listened. The enjoyment of two people spending their time together without the necessity of a deeper commitment.

Was he perhaps still loyal to Mary, feeling her loss too deeply, in spite of what he had once said, to enable him to fall in love with another woman? Or did Miranda mean something in his life? Whatever it was, her thoughts were a factor that caused unhappiness in the midst of Emma's joy at spending so much of her time with him.

And joy there was. She cherished the hours when she sat beside Stewart in the jeep, while he went about his work. More and more she was getting an insight into all his work entailed, and to respect the men who dedicated their lives to the thousands of animals in the vast sanctuary.

The day at the dam had only been one small part of it all. Emma began to learn how the rangers were able to identify the various herds of animals, and how they were able to compute their numbers. She learnt of the precautions taken to prevent fires, and of the ever-pressing need to find water supplies. For water was the precious factor in the Park, the elixir of life on which all else depended.

She learnt too about the poachers, the scourge of the game rangers.

Stewart was talking of them now as they drove along the road that led south to Malelane, and while he spoke she turned in her seat to look at him. The strong profile was turned away from her, his eyes searching the bush, and she was able to watch him and wonder at his thoughts.

'They're an absolute menace,' he said. 'If I had my way I'd round up every man who ever poached and set his foot in a snare, then watch his despair as he hopped about in agony while he tried to free himself.'

'Are there so many poachers, then?' she asked.

'A fair amount. Every now and then they get frightened off and things are quiet for a while, and then, when they think themselves safe, it all starts up again.'

'Why do they poach?' She thought of traps set in woods in England, traps to ensnare rabbits and other animals that would make delicacies for the pot, but she was puzzled at the thought of poaching in the Park.

'They trap buck, for one thing. Buck makes good biltong and fetches a high price.' Emma knew what biltong was, the meat that was dried and cut in long sticks and was such a delicacy. 'Elephant tusks mean ivory, and some animals are valuable for their skins. Oh, there are plenty of markets for the poacher.'

'How do they do it, Stewart?' she asked. 'Aren't they frightened?' For it had been a source of wonder to her whenever she caught a glimpse, as she occasionally did, of a man walking through the bush. 'What about lions?'

'I shouldn't tell you this, I know.' He was smiling now and mischief twinkled behind his eyes. 'Because if I do you'll be right there in the bush taking pictures whenever the angle from the car is not satisfactory.'

'You're not going to tell me the animals are circus-trained, after all?' She pretended to pout. These were the moments she cherished, the moments when they were at ease with each other, lighthearted and teasing.

'You'd never forgive me if I did that, would you?' He was laughing, and it was all she could do to restrain herself from moving closer beside him, stretching out a hand to touch the rumpled hair.

'No,' she said, pretending to consider the matter carefully, 'I don't think I would. It would break my heart to think how many lovely shots I'd been done out of.'

'Then in that case I won't chance my arm. No,' he went on, more seriously now, 'you really can't get out of your car and go walking an inch into the bush. But the people who live here, they can do it. Though even they sometimes make a mistake, and when that happens' – he made an expressive gesture. 'But these people who have grown up here, who have lived all their lives in and around the Park, they know the lions and understand their ways. They know when the lions are hungry and when they're likely to make a kill. And at those times they would not be so foolish as to venture along the roads on foot. But they also know that the lion only kills when he's hungry.'

'I didn't know that,' said Emma.

'There are many things you don't know, little one.' Again he was laughing down at her. 'And it's one of the things I shouldn't be telling you too much about. But it's true that lions kill only when they're hungry. Of course, there *are* predators which do kill just for the thrill of it – tigers, for instance. But we don't have tigers in Africa.'

'So then there are really times when it's safe to be in the bush?'

'There are. Though perhaps it's never very wise. Emma, haven't you seen how a herd of buck will stay sometimes at a water-hole even when a lion approaches?'

'I *have* seen that, and I thought perhaps it was just foolishness.'

'Not at all – just the opposite. Animals know when the lion has eaten. They know when a kill was made, and that there won't be another for several days. They know when the lion can lie down with the lamb,' he smiled.

'So that's why the poachers know when they can walk through the bush.'

'The poachers? Yes.' The laughter died behind his eyes, and his expression became set and grim. 'They've done a lot of harm around here lately.'

'There's something I don't understand, Stewart. How do you know when they've snared an animal? If they take it away with them, would you be any the wiser?'

'These people set snares. At first they clear them regularly. Then, when they don't happen to need the animals, they forget about the snares they've left in the bush. Animals get trapped, nobody comes, and they're left in agony.'

'But how horrible!' she shuddered.

'It is,' he agreed. 'And it's one of the things we try to stamp out. There are heavy penalties for poaching, but the rewards are high, so there are always men who will try it.'

'It's all so senseless, isn't it?' Emma was silent a while, thinking how people could react so differently to animals. On the one hand there were the game rangers, the conservationists, Stewart and his colleagues, who wanted only to help, to protect the game, to save them from the ravages of drought and the many other dangers that could befall them. And on the other hand there were the poachers and the hunters, to whom killing of game could mean fun or profit, who were completely insensitive to

123

the agony and distress that they caused.

'It is senseless,' he agreed grimly. 'And we're in the throes of it at the moment.'

'I didn't know that,' she said wonderingly, realizing once again how much went on in this vast sanctuary of which tourists were unaware.

'We've been suspecting it for some time. We'd been hearing rumours. And then in the last few weeks there have been reports of badly injured animals – animals that are starving, and unable to find food because of their injuries.'

'What do you do when you find these animals?' she asked.

'We put them out of their misery,' he said briefly, and his face was still and stern as he stared in front of him. 'We track them down. Often it takes days to find the animal, but we go on until we find it, and then we try to deal mercifully with it.'

'This trip today,' she ventured tentatively. 'Has this something to do with poaching?'

'I'm afraid so.' He was silent a moment. When he continued his voice was cold and composed, the voice Emma had learnt to associate with anger. 'There have been reports of elephants that have been snared.'

'Elephants?' she gasped.

'They seem to have worked their way free from the traps,' he went on, ignoring her exclamation, 'but not entirely. They've been injured. One elephant has been sighted with a snare wound around its trunk.'

'Oh, no!' She was horrified, thinking of the animal's pain.

'Do you know what that means?' He turned to look at her.

'It must be in pain . . .'

'Pain, yes. But worse than that. The animal is starving.

Soon it could die.'

'Why, Stewart?'

'Because without the use of its trunk it can't get food. It can breathe through its mouth, but it can't do without its trunk. It needs it to gather food.'

'Oh, Stewart, how terrible!'

'Sometimes when this happens the elephant tries to drag the snare off its trunk by forcing it against the trees, but usually it only makes the injuries worse.' He was still speaking in the same expressionless voice. 'We must find that elephant.'

'How . . .?'

'The rangers and the trackers have been out for days now. You probably noticed that I haven't been around the last few days.' She had, and had wondered at his absence. 'We've been out in the bush, trying to trace the elephant's spoor.'

'And have you found the spoor?'

'We can't be certain – there are so many elephants. But until we find it we must go on.'

'Why have you brought me here today?' she asked.

'Because I'm not in the bush today. I've come to gather information from various rangers and to take it back again. I wish' – he struck his forehead in a futile gesture – 'I wish to God we'd find the animal. It can't go on much longer like this.'

'What will happen if you don't find it?'

'I try not to think about that. We'll go on looking until we do.' He was silent for a moment, and again she was struck by his sense of dedication. 'Did you know, Emma, that the elephants could put the poor beast out of its agony?'

'I don't understand,' she said.

'Sometimes, when one of their number is very sick, they'll help it to find food. And when an elephant is injured, badly injured, so badly injured that they know that he must die, they'll kill him to end his agony.'

She looked at him in wonder, and he went on, more quietly now, but with more emotion in his voice, 'It's rather wonderful, really. There's so much about the animals that we don't know. There's so much that they seem to sense, just by instinct. So many of their actions have logic behind them. Perhaps it's just the logic of instinct. But when an elephant gets killed by the herd there's a reason – not like humans, who kill just for the fun of it.'

At Malelane Emma walked about while Stewart went about his business. After a while she saw him looking for her and walked to join him.

'I'd treat you to lunch,' he said, 'but I must get back. Do you mind if we just have something light and get on our way?'

'Of course not.'

'It's not the right way to treat you. It's deathly hot, I know, and you haven't had much of a morning . . .'

'It's all right, Stewart. Really it is,' she said swiftly, wishing she could tell him that all she wanted was to be near him, and that all else was of no importance.

'Thank you, Emma.' He smiled at her, then wiped a hand across his brow, and she could see how tired he was. 'You're very understanding. Perhaps when all this is over I'll be able to make it up to you.'

They were on their way back to Skukuza when he said, 'There's a film tomorrow night.'

'Oh?' She looked at him expectantly. Every few days the camp showed a film for the visitors, and it was always an event to be looked forward to. It was usually a wild-life film, and it would be shown out in the open, which seemed to make it rather special.

'Will you come with me?' he asked.

'I'd love to,' she said, and he took a hand from the wheel and patted hers briefly, and Emma felt all at once very happy.

The hot dusty miles fell away, and they sat together without speaking, in a silence that was more companionable than speech. Stewart drove steadily and well, never exceeding the speed limit, but not going too slowly either as he had to get back to camp. Nevertheless, every now and then, in deference to her, he slowed down when there was something special to see.

This was what she loved, this driving quietly and with a feeling of harmony between them. She knew now that she never could tire of this life. It had gripped her senses and her imagination as nothing else had in her life before. But she knew too that if Stewart did not ask her to stay she would have to leave when the three months were over. There would be no excuse for her to linger, and she could not live for ever as a tourist.

Only a few more weeks left now. She thought as little as possible of the time when this idyll must come to an end, and when the thought did enter her mind she tried to banish it, for it was one that had become unendurable.

Even if Lance were to propose to her, and once or twice he had laughingly hinted that he intended to do so, she knew she could not use this as an excuse to stay. Indeed, she would have to refuse him for that very reason, because allied to the fact that she did not love him and therefore did not want to marry him was the knowledge that she could not live in the Park with Lance, as his wife, and watch the man she really loved going about his work. There would be an air of finality about that which would be worse than leaving here and knowing she would never see him again.

CHAPTER EIGHT

EMMA hung around the camp for a little while the next morning, hoping that she might see Stewart, and that he might ask her to accompany him again. But he was no-where to be seen. Slowly she sauntered through the personnel quarters, down to the river, and then back through the shop.

She was walking through the shop when she saw Lance and she called out cheerfully, 'Hello. How are things with you this morning?'

'All the better for seeing you, sweetheart. Not out on the roads yet?'

'No. I'll go presently, but I was feeling a little lazy today.'

'If you're looking for Stewart' – he was looking at her with an oddly amused expression – 'he's not here.'

'Oh!' She was confused at his bluntness. 'I . . . I wasn't looking for him.'

'Sorry, poppet, I thought that's what you spent quite a lot of your time doing.'

'Heavens, Lance!' She was annoyed, wondering at the same time whether her feelings were really so trans-parent. 'I think I can decide how to spend my days with-out you jumping to conclusions.'

'Okay, sweetheart.' He was mocking her again. 'No need for one of those Women's Lib speeches. I'd be only too glad if I thought you weren't worrying about Stewart's whereabouts.'

'I'm not,' she repeated with exasperation. 'Look, can we change the subject?'

'Surely. If you *do* decide to make a day of it, don't tire

yourself out.'

'Why not?'

'There's a film on tonight.'

'Oh!' She was immediately on her guard.

'Will you come with me, Emma?'

'I can't, Lance, I'm sorry.'

'You already have a date?'

She nodded.

'Stewart?'

'. . . Yes.'

'I see.' Lance's face was suddenly stiff and cold and the bantering mood was gone. 'All right, Emma. Be seeing you around.' He turned and went back to his work, and Emma, annoyed with his childishness, walked out of the shop.

Slowly she went back to the spot by the river which she had grown to love so much. She leaned her elbows on the fence, cupped her chin in her hands, staring thoughtfully into the bush. For once she was not searching for game, but was more absorbed in pondering over Lance's words. Was it becoming obvious to others the way she felt about Stewart? Did Stewart himself know and think the less of her for it? Was she, in fact, becoming obsessed?

So absorbed was she in her thoughts that she was unaware of anyone near her till she heard a voice say, 'Hello, Emma.'

'Johnny!' She turned and her eyes lit with the pleasure she always felt when she saw the boy. 'I didn't hear you coming.'

'I know. You were what my mother calls "in another world".'

'I'm back now,' she said briskly. 'And about time too. Well, Johnny, feel like coming for a drive?'

'I'd like that,' he said eagerly.

'Will it be all right if we meet at my car in about ten

minutes?'

She went to her room, and as she collected her cameras she looked at the painting that hung above her bed, and at the plant that stood on the table. Was the plant merely a gift that had been given thoughtlessly and on the spur of the moment? Was she reading more into the gift than had been intended?

She shrugged her shoulders impatiently, as if she were trying to shake away the feelings of insecurity that Lance had, as he so often did, managed to implant. And, she asked herself, trying to be objective, was Lance at fault? Had he done anything wrong? Had he implied more than his words said? Or was it just that her own feelings of doubt left her wide open to any negative suggestions?

She slung her cameras over her shoulders, placed a piece of biltong into her bag, and went to meet Johnny.

As always the sight of the cheerful freckled face dispelled any bad humour, and with a smile at him she drove out of the camp.

'Where will it be today, Johnny?'

'Anywhere,' he said nonchalantly.

'Fibber!' She turned to him, laughing. 'I see a pencil sticking out of that bulky pocket of yours. And that couldn't be a sketch-pad in there, could it?'

'I can never fool you,' he said, and he was laughing too.

'To the hippo-pool we'll go, then.' By the time they were half-way there, the boy chatting ingenuously at her side, Emma's good spirits had been restored.

'How is the painting going?' she asked once.

'Pretty well. I've filled in quite a bit of detail. But there's still a lot that needs doing.'

'Well, you know I like going to the hippo-pool. It's one of my favourite spots. And I'm sure your dad has more important things to occupy him.'

'Yes ... Especially at the moment.' His face puckered in a frown. 'They've gone after the elephant that was snared.'

'I heard about that,' said Emma. 'Has it been found?'

'Not yet, though they think they're on his trail. They've gone after him again today.'

'Who is "they", Johnny?'

'A whole crowd of rangers and trackers.'

'Your dad?'

'Yes, Dad is there. And Stewart too.'

'Oh!' She breathed out the word on a sigh.

'That's why I'm not with Dad today,' Johnny explained. 'They left early. Part of the way will be on foot through the bush. Dad says I'm too young to join in that sort of thing.'

And I'm too inexperienced. And a female besides. Emma did not speak the words. But she was glad to know the reason why Stewart had left her behind today, though at the same time she worried about his safety. 'Do you think they'll find the elephant and track it down today?' she asked.

'Gosh, I hope so.' Behind the boy's twelve-year-old eyes was much of the experience and wisdom and caring of a game ranger. He might want to be an artist, Emma reflected, but there was, nevertheless, a lot in him of his father.

'And when they find the elephant – what will they do?'

'I guess that depends on what they find,' said Johnny.

They spent a restful day at the hippo-pool. While Johnny sketched, Emma sat on the rocky outcrop, listening absentmindedly to his chatter, and enjoying the feeling of the sun upon her face and limbs.

Although she came here mainly to please the boy, the hippo-pool had, in fact, become one of her favourite spots. It was very beautiful, fringed by shady trees, and with big black rocks near the water. Often the hippos lay submerged beneath the water, but she had seen them sometimes, on the far bank of the pool, ambling somnambulently along, clumsy, amiable-looking creatures.

She remembered the first time Johnny had brought her here, and how nervous she had been to get out of the car, expecting that at any moment a lion might jump out at them from behind a bush. But Johnny had shown her the sign saying that it was safe to leave the car, and later Stewart had confirmed what the boy had said, that no predators came there. Why and how they could be sure of this, she did not know, but they had explained to her that hundreds of visitors alighted from their cars at this point every year, and that there were never any casualties.

It was late afternoon when they got back to camp. Emma wondered whether the game rangers had come back, but when Johnny went to find his father, he returned with the news that the men were still away. The gate would be closing soon, and in all probability they would be spending the night at one of the other camps.

Emma was aware of bitter disappointment. She had been looking forward to spending the evening with Stewart. Also, she wondered whether he was safe. 'Would you like to have a braai with me, Johnny?' she asked the boy.

'Gosh, Emma, I'd like that, but Mom is waiting for me.'

Emma did not feel in the mood to go to much trouble when she prepared her supper that evening, and she had a quick meal. All about her she could see the little fires beginning to glow, could smell the tantalizing aroma of the meat, could hear the excited chatter of children. All at once she felt lonely and somehow excluded. The camps in the Park seemed intended for groups – young people travelling together, tours, mainly families. A girl all on her own could feel out of things.

She could hear children chattering excitedly, looking forward to the film. Now that Emma knew Stewart would not be back she hardly felt like going. Lance, of course, had invited her to sit with him, but if she approached him now it would seem as if she were making do with second best. For a while she thought she would stay in her room and have an early night.

When she had finished her meagre supper she washed her utensils and walked for a while around the camp. The atmosphere was exhilarating. Because of the film people were finishing their supper more quickly than usual. Soon children, in pyjamas and gowns, and their parents with rugs and cushions, began drifting towards the big open-air clearing where the screen stood in readiness.

As she watched the activity around her, Emma began to realize how foolish she was being. The film would be shown in an atmosphere of extreme informality, with people squatting on the ground, or sitting on camp-stools. It was not a formal screening in a cinema, where one had to book a ticket and walk to one's seat, and where one might feel conspicuous to be alone.

Here nobody would give her a second glance. Besides, if people were really beginning to read into her emotions, as Lance had insinuated, her absence from the scene would make her feelings even more obvious to anyone who might know her.

She remembered the decision she had made on her first day at Skukuza, and she reproached herself for even having considered missing an event that meant so much in the life of the camp, only because the man she had planned to spend it with would not be there.

Finding a place in the open-air auditorium, she sat down and made herself comfortable, looking around her with interest and amusement. Though it was not the first time there had been a film – they were shown fairly often – there was about them always an air of expectation and excitement which she loved.

All at once she became aware of someone standing over her and she looked up. It was Lance. 'All alone?' he asked, his eyebrows raised quizzically.

'Yes.'

'Been let down by your young man?'

'Oh, Lance, you're impossible!' She laughed up at him, determined not to get into an argument. 'Stewart went out after the injured elephant today. I don't suppose he knew he'd be away when he mentioned the film yesterday.'

'Hm.' Lance looked at her thoughtfully. 'Well, whatever else my vices might be, I'm not one to hold grudges. May I join you?'

'Of course.' She was glad when he sat down. In spite of her resolve not to back out of the film just because she was alone, she knew it was more fun to be there in company. And she liked Lance. Despite his occasional childishness he was friendly and pleasant, and so handsome with the flash of white teeth in the quick bright smile. 'I'd love you to sit here,' she said.

She saw that he carried a rug. 'Get up a minute,' he said, and when she did so, he spread the rug on the ground beneath them. 'More çomfortable?' he asked.

'Much more,' she smiled, and all of a sudden she knew she was going to enjoy the evening.

At last the film began. It was a documentary showing life in a beehive, and after this film there were two others.

Emma had had a long day, and the one before that had been long too, and Emma had not realized how tired she was. Despite her enjoyment of the films she found that her eyes felt like lead, and that her head was beginning to droop. 'I think I'll go to bed, Lance,' she said.

'And leave me all alone?'

'Oh, Lance, I'm so tired!'

'Go on, Emma, please stay. You'll get a second wind just now. Stay here. Be a sport!'

'Oh . . . all right, but it's chilly. I think I'll go and get a cardigan. I'll be back in a moment.'

'No need,' said Lance, detaining her as she was about to stand. 'We'll do what everybody else is doing. Bend that way a moment.' He drew the rug from under her and, deftly managing to leave enough on the ground for her to sit on, drew it around her shoulders. 'Snug?' he asked her.

'Mm.'

'Well, that's good. And if you get tired you can lean your head against my shoulder and doze for a little. Nobody will see, and my shoulder is strong.'

'You're a dear, Lance,' she said gratefully, as the next film was beginning.

She leaned towards him and rested her head against his shoulder, keeping her eyes open as she tried to concentrate on the film. It was an interesting film, and though she felt her fatigue begin to catch up with her, she was determined not to sleep. She only leaned against him because it was somehow less of a strain, and in a way, it was cosy and comfortable. Once she caught her eyes closing and forced them open.

She did not know it when she fell asleep. When she awoke the film was finished, her head was still comfortably pillowed against Lance, but it had dropped a little, and she found herself lying against his chest. And towering over them stood a man. Stewart!

'Oh!' she gasped, sitting bolt upright. And when he

said nothing, 'Stewart! I thought you hadn't come back.'

'So I see,' he said grimly.

'Stewart . . .' She knew how the scene must appear to him, as he stood there looking down at them, huddled together beneath the rug, her head against Lance's chest.

'Yes?'

'I know I said I'd come with you, but you weren't here . . . and I was all alone, and Lance came to sit with me . . .' She stopped, aware that she was only making the situation more complex, and therefore worse. Besides, she thought with a sudden flash of annoyance, why was she apologizing? She had done nothing wrong. It was bad tactics, she had once been told, to apologize when one was not at fault. It was like admitting to fault.

'I don't know what we're all getting so upset about,' she said a little angrily.

'You're the only one who's getting upset,' Stewart observed quietly. 'I don't think I said anything – nor did Lance.'

'It's the way you look – as if I'd done something wrong. I looked for you, but I thought you weren't back.'

'We got back very late, after the gates were officially closed.'

'Then I couldn't have known. And . . . and then I didn't see you.'

'I had things to discuss.'

'Oh . . . the elephant.' She remembered it now, too late. 'Did you find it?'

'Yes, we found it.'

'Was it all right?'

'Half its trunk had been torn away by the snare. It was in bad shape.' He spoke calmly and unemotionally in the way she hated.

'What did you do?' she asked.

'We shot it.'

'Oh, how dreadful . . . how dreadful!' She put her hand before her mouth.

'Yes.' He looked at them both a moment longer, unemotionally, impersonally, a perfect stranger. Then he bade them good night and walked away.

'Well,' observed Lance, when Stewart had gone, 'he's charming, your swain.'

'What do you mean?' She looked at him unhappily.

'Not a very good loser, is he?'

'Yes . . . No . . . I *had* promised to be with him tonight,' she explained.

'But you thought he wasn't here. And you didn't want to go alone.'

'That's right.'

'So you turned to me, the standby.'

'Oh, Lance!' She turned to him swiftly, shocked by the bitterness in his voice. 'That's not what happened.'

'It's all I've ever been, isn't it? A standby.'

'That's not true. You know it isn't.'

'Isn't it, Emma? Isn't it?'

She looked at him, knowing that what he said was partially true. She liked him, and enjoyed his company, but her feelings for Lance and those for Stewart could not be compared. You could love only one man. All others could be friends – good friends, but only friends.

'It sounds so awful, the way you say it,' she sighed at last.

'But it's true?'

'No, Lance, not the way you put it. I've never thought of you as a standby.'

'But you don't love me.' It was a statement rather than a question. 'Pity about that, Emma, it really is. Because you love a man who will never love you. I warned you about that the first day. Remember?'

Emma did not answer. She stood up, shook the grass from her slacks, hugged her arms about her, and said, 'I think it's time I went to bed, Lance. Are you walking my way?'

'You know I am. I've got a tin of cocoa with me, and two mugs. We'll stop at one of the urns and I'll make us each a cup of cocoa. Just what we need at this time of night, now that it's turned so chilly.'

'You have two mugs?' She stared at him. 'But you didn't know I was going to be with you. Did you, Lance?'

He did not answer immediately, but looked down at her, his eyes unreadable in the darkness. 'I was hoping,' he said at last.

'Lance, did you know . . . did you know Stewart was back?'

'How should I have known?' he said easily. 'Well, Emma, is the fact that I have an extra cup with me going to be held as an indictment?'

'Of course not.'

'Then you'll have a cup of cocoa?'

'Thank you, Lance, I'd like that.'

The cocoa, when they drank it, was warm and sweet, and she felt it course through her body like a thin stream of fire. 'That was nice,' she said when they walked to a tap together, and rinsed the cups. 'And now I think it's really time to say good night.'

She undressed quickly, for it was cold by now, and then, when she had her pyjamas on, she sat down on the bed and looked at the pot-plant that stood on the little table. At last she slid beneath the blankets, and reached up and switched off the light.

For some time she lay sleepless, listening to the sounds that come with the night. Outside the world rang with the

138

chirping of millions of crickets, and above that sound, the sound of Africa at night, came the sounds of animals. Once an elephant trumpeted, and once the roar of a lion bounded through the bush, low, mighty, unmistakable.

Slowly the sounds of the camp subsided, the laughter, the chatter, the singing of people at camp-fires. Soon all was still, only the crickets and the mingled sounds of wild life merging together. And still Emma lay awake.

What had Stewart thought when he had found them tonight? It had all been so innocent, so very innocent. She had been alone, as Lance had been, and they had decided to sit together. Lance had had a rug with him, just as all the other people there had had, because it grew chilly in the bush when the sun was gone. She was tired, and he had let her rest against him, like a child resting against its father for comfort.

Only Lance was not a parent and she, Emma, was not a child. Lance was a man, a good-looking, pleasant, fun-to-be-with man. And Emma was a woman. And Lance was jealous – this much she knew now.

So the analogy was not altogether right. She had rested against him for comfort, but she was not a child, and Lance was not a parent. And Stewart – Stewart, too, was a man.

She saw again the two cups which Lance had filled with cocoa, the cups which he had produced so easily from his pocket, and again her suspicions rose.

Had he known Stewart was back? Had he known Stewart was busy discussing what had happened that day, but would be around later to claim her? It was absurd, of course. Even Johnny had not known the men were back. But she felt, she knew somehow, that Lance had known. Her last thought before going to sleep took the shape of a question – if Lance *had* known, why had he behaved as he did?

139

CHAPTER NINE

When unpleasant things happened they never came singly, Emma had discovered.

Three days after the fiasco at the film, Linda Willis had a party. Linda was the wife of one of the game rangers, and she had decided to celebrate her birthday. She invited all the staff at the camp, and because Emma, by virtue of her long stay at the Park, had become accepted as one of them, she was invited too.

Emma's mind was not on wild-life on the day of Linda's party. It was silly, and she knew it, but she wondered ceaselessly whether she should go. At one moment she thought she would refuse. She could plead a headache or a mild case of sunstroke. And then, the next moment, she would reproach herself for her foolishness, reminding herself of her resolve to be strong, and not to show that she cared. All day she vacillated, and then, in the later afternoon, sitting at the water-hole by the river which Stewart had shown her, she realized how silly she was being.

There was no reason why she should stay away from the party. If Stewart was annoyed because she had been at the film with Lance, then he was the one who was being childish, and there was nothing she could do about it. After all, it was not as if she had deliberately sought out Lance's company. If Stewart had been there she would have gone with him as arranged.

And how could she have known he was back? She could not have known – yet always at the back of her mind was the gnawing suspicion that Lance had known, and that he had coaxed her into leaning against him with the rug about them both just because he had wanted to provoke an incident.

Men! They said women were incomprehensible, that it was impossible to know why a woman spoke or acted as she did. Yet it was men who were the strange ones – impossible creatures, jealous, demanding and ambivalent. It was strange that much as she had decided to keep clear of any emotional entanglement in Africa, somehow, without volition, she had succeeded in doing the opposite.

Emma thought again about the party. She knew she was looking well. Stewart would recognize the pretext of a headache for an excuse, while Lance would take pleasure in rubbing it in.

She would go. She would go to the party, and to blazes with them both. Perhaps, she thought with a spark of devilment, she would find a third man to spend the evening with, and put Stewart's nose out of joint, and that of Lance as well.

Once she had decided to go to the party the problem remained what to wear. Not that her evening wardrobe was extensive. For wear in the Park she had brought with her a long cotton skirt with a simple blouse, and a pale blue dress that she had worn sometimes to parties in England. She knew she could safely wear either of these outfits.

Or she could wear the pink dress. Sometimes, before she went to bed at night, she would take out the dress and lay it on her bed. Caressing the soft folds of the material, she would relive the lovely evenings she had spent with Stewart. Then there had been harmony between them, as well as something more.

Now – now he was angry with her, unjustifiably angry, cold and matter-of-fact. Sometimes Emma wished he would seek her out and give vent to his anger. Even if it meant having a scene, if it meant shouting back at him, at least she could have explained things and put the matter right. But there was only the coldness when they chanced to meet, the scrupulous politeness, the manner of a stranger.

At length she decided that she would wear the cotton skirt and the blouse to the party. She would dress her hair a little differently, and on her face would be the smile of a person with not a care in the world.

Emma came back to camp a little earlier that afternoon. Before going to have a shower she opened the little cupboard, looked at the pink dress and fingered it thoughtfully. Then she took the skirt and blouse and laid them out on her bed.

When she returned from the shower her hair was moist and curling, and her skin was aglow from the sun and from the rough towelling she had given it. She brushed her hair and put on a little lipstick. Then she dressed herself. When she was ready she looked at herself in the mirror, and from there she walked to the pot-plant. All at once she shook her head. Hurriedly she took off the blouse and the skirt, hung them back in the cupboard, and then taking the pink dress from its hanger slipped it over her head.

She glanced at her watch. It was time to go.

'Emma!' Lance was the first to see her. 'You look – you look very beautiful.' The smile that lit his face was neither as quick not as mechanical as usual, and it seemed to her that there was more meaning in it. 'Very beautiful indeed.'

'Thank you.' And then she was looking past at him, and at Stewart, and he too was looking at her, not with the stranger's face that he had worn these last three days, nor yet with the face she had seen in Pretoria, but with a gravity, a thoughtfulness which she could not understand.

'Stewart . . .' He put out a hand to her, and she was about to go up to him, when a woman joined them – a very beautiful woman: Miranda.

'You two have met, haven't you?' The look on Stewart's face was gone, and his eyes were impersonal again.

'Yes, of course. How are you, Miranda?' Emma was smiling, but behind her eyes, where nobody could see, she knew she was crying. Miranda was standing beside Stewart now, and he made no attempt to detach himself as she drew her arm through his.

'Of course we've met,' said Miranda. 'The little photographer. I hadn't realized you were still here.'

'Oh, yes, I'm still around.'

'Will you be here much longer?' The tone was casual, but to her astonishment Emma realized that the question was loaded with meaning. Was it possible that even Miranda was not sure of her position? That she too felt feelings of insecurity?

Fortunately they were not left to talk together for long. Linda had her party prepared, and soon the visitors were gathered around the fires, laughing and talking.

Though a braai was a commonplace event in camp-life, Linda had been to much trouble, and managed to endow the proceedings with a certain amount of festivity. The food was set out on a long table. There were platters with meat; chops and juicy steaks, and *boerewors*. In addition, she had prepared kebabs, which, Emma learnt, were another South African speciality; skewers with cubes of lamb and onion and green peppers speared on to them. There were mealies, slightly boiled, and only waiting for a roasting to make them special. There were potatoes, cooked in their jackets, and long slivers of cucumber and tomatoes and spears of asparagus. It was all the fare of a camp-fire, at its best and most delicious.

Soon the fire had died to a heap of glowing embers, and

was ready for the meat. As the men laid the long forks on the grids, forks heavy with steak and *boerewors* and spicy kebabs, the fat dripped from the meat and hit the glowing flames with a crackle, and a mouth-watering aroma wafted through the air.

Jokes and laughter began to fly around the fires. Most of these people knew one another well, and though they met often there was something about the easy, happy informality of the party that loosened tongues and set the eyes to smiling.

Miranda still stood with Stewart, her hand clutching at his arm, and Emma was glad when Lance came to her, carrying two cardboard plates in one hand, and doing a balancing trick with cool drink glasses in the other.

'Let me enjoy this,' Emma pleaded with herself. 'This is what I came for – to eat beneath the star-studded African sky, with the cries of wild beasts sounding through the darkness, while a man plays an accordion and the crickets sing. This is why I left England. For fun and laughter in a different setting, away from rain and mist, away from unhappiness and broken promises, away from complications and recriminations. Away from love.'

When they had finished eating they began to dance. In another set of circumstances, on a different night, and with another man's arms around her waist, Emma would have been in heaven.

The lovely smell of exotic shrubs mingled with the tantalizing aromas of the braai. There was the vastness of the sky above, the murmur of people, and beyond, where the fence separated the light and laughter from the darkness of the wilds, came the intermittent sounds of the animals, sometimes harsh, always harmonious in this setting. This was what Emma had dreamed of when she had left England, and normally the atmosphere at this party would have set her tingling with exhilaration.

As it was she felt flat. The anticipation, the small hope always at the back of her mind that Stewart would come back to her, that hope which had provoked the wearing of the pink dress, had now gone. Inexplicably the sight of the visitors enjoying themselves served only to heighten her own sense of anti-climax.

'Relax, Emma,' Lance said once. 'You're as tense as a cat about to spring.'

'I'm sorry,' she said contritely, allowing him to draw her closer into his arms. Dear Lance! He had been so good to her, so kind from the first day she had arrived at the camp. Always patient and understanding, friendly and smiling. Sometimes he had shown disappointment when he saw that she preferred Stewart's company to his own, but the ill feeling had never lasted long.

He was always there, always in the background. The second fiddle ready to take the part of the first when the need arose, she thought irrelevantly. And though she tried to suppress the thought as soon as it arose, she knew that it was true. Lance was the second fiddle in her life, and no matter what happened, no matter whether Stewart returned her love or not, this was the way it would always be.

She leaned closer towards him when she saw it was what he wanted, as if by complying she could make up for the injustice she was doing him in her mind. But at the same time she was glad when Lance held her close. For not far away she saw Stewart and Miranda. They too were dancing together, and she watched as Miranda flung her head back once, laughing up at Stewart, obviously amused at something he had said, while he in turn laughed back at her. Then, the shared joke at an end, she put her head on his shoulder, and the hand that rested on his arm went up about his neck.

Somewhere inside Emma, buried deep below the

145

façade that laughed and smiled and joked, there was a pain that twisted and tore. The pressure of Lance's arm about her waist, the hardness of his shoulder against her chin, the very humanness and the feeling that someone cared, in some small measure helped her, not to lessen the pain, but to make it bearable.

They had been dancing a while when there was a pause for refreshments. Presently the music started again. Lance turned casually to her and said, 'Would you mind if I left you for a little while, Emma?'

'Of course not.'

'I want to have the next dance with Miranda.'

For a moment Emma stared at him in astonishment. Then she quickly pulled herself together and said, 'Of course I don't mind. You know that.'

She watched him walk over to where Stewart and Miranda stood together, watched them stop talking as he came up to them, saw Miranda glance up at Stewart and say a few words. Then she moved into Lance's arms. Emma watched it all, as if it were a dream sequence, and then she saw Stewart pause, and look after them a moment, before he moved in her direction.

Then the dream was ended, and she felt her mouth go dry as she looked about her as if to find someone to talk to, some means of escape. This was not what she wanted – that Stewart should feel obliged to ask her to dance because she was standing alone. An obligation. A duty.

'Don't run away from me, Emma.' The deep voice was close behind her.

'I'm not running . . . I . . .' she faltered, looking back at him.

'You looked as if you were. Will you dance with me, Emma?'

'Yes.' She was in his arms then, moving to the beat of the music, and for a little while she felt as if she were back with him on that other dance-floor, as if nothing had ever happened.

Then she remembered Miranda, and realized that he had asked her to dance only because the other girl was with Lance. The spell was broken. Instead of moving in silence, enjoying the music and the feel of his arms around her, she felt impelled all of a sudden to talk. But the talk was not natural, the spontaneous expression of all that she really wanted to say. Rather it was the forced chatter of a stranger, bright, brittle and gay.

'Isn't this super fun?' she heard herself saying.

'You're enjoying it?'

'Oh, it's just the greatest. Linda's a marvellous hostess. Such lovely food and . . . and everything. And of course, Lance – I've been dancing with him most of the evening, you know – he's such a darling. Just the right kind of person with whom to spend such an evening.'

'You sound like a piece of advertising copy, Emma,' Stewart commented dryly.

'Oh, but he *is* super. Don't you think so? He's . . . he's a fun person. Don't you agree?' Stewart did not answer, and she found herself babbling on and on, empty chatter, exuberant and exaggerated, totally without meaning. But she could not stop. She had to prevent silences before they could become embarrassing. And all the while, as she prattled, something within her was weeping.

Presently the dance was over. Stewart thanked her and as he moved away from her, smiling politely and impersonally, she knew that with this duty dance, anything else that might have existed between them was also at an end. The hope that she and Stewart might make things up tonight had been futile. If anything, she was further from him now than she had ever been.

Lance danced with her once more, and she was glad of the comfort his arms gave to her. They danced together quietly. The need to talk, to fill the silences, was gone. And though she was only half aware of it, Lance too had fallen strangely silent.

Later that evening, when the sounds of the camp had stilled, and the guests at the party had said their good-byes, Lance took Emma for a last stroll around the camp.

It was near the river that she saw them – the tall figure and the small one, he with his arm around her waist, she with her face turned up to his. Involuntarily Emma stopped still, and Lance stopped walking too. As they watched, Stewart suddenly bent, put his other arm around Miranda, and kissed her. It was over quickly, but Lance and Emma turned and walked the other way.

She glanced up at Lance, half expecting to see on his face the look of satisfaction she had seen there on the night of the film, when Stewart had found her leaning against him with the rug about them both for warmth. That look was not there this time. Strangely, in its place was an expression that seemed compounded of bitterness and resignation and unhappiness. Had Emma not been so occupied with her own feelings of despair she might have questioned that expression in her mind. As it was, she shrugged it off and forgot about it.

To Emma's surprise, a few days after the party, Stewart asked her to go out with him. He had business, he said, at one of the other camps, and thought she might like to accompany him.

The day began pleasantly enough, with no overt strife or conflict of any kind. Indeed, in a way Emma wished there had been conflict of some sort, for it might have brought with it a clearing of the air, and so an end to the tension that lurked beneath the surface friendliness between them. It could have ended the polite barrier of strangers who seemed to say, 'This we will talk of, but not that. This far we will venture, but not further.'

They talked and laughed together, but Emma was continually aware of that tension, of the need to avoid silence, for she sensed that silence, at this point, would be unbearable. While they talked they were careful to avoid any topic that might lead to argument. Lance's name was not mentioned, nor that of Miranda. The film and the party were as if they had never been.

Emma could not relax, so conscious was she of this feeling between them, as tangible as if it were made of bricks. Did Stewart feel it too? she wondered.

They came in the late afternoon to a water-hole. It was one that Emma had not previously been to. It lay on a ranger's road, a road that tourists never saw, and Emma enjoyed the peace and beauty of the sun-dappled clearing, with the river and the hoofmarked sand just below them.

In the shade of the trees, sheltering from the sun, which even now in the later afternoon, still burned hotly, was a herd of impala. Though she had been in the Park for so long now, and knew the impala to be one of its most plentiful animals, Emma still thrilled to its effortless grace, the ever-present look of newly-washed freshness, the delicate pose of the head and the alertness of the lovely liquid eyes.

'Some people say humans remind them of animals,' she observed to Stewart as she watched them.

'Which group do I fit into?' he asked, with an amused quirk at the corner of his mouth.

'Egoist!' she laughed, side-stepping the question. 'I wasn't thinking of you.' If she had to choose an animal to represent Stewart which one would it be? Which one would best symbolize the arrogance that could turn to gentleness, and the fiercely independent spirit? 'I was

149

really thinking that some animals are like people,' she said.

'Reverse thinking.' His eyes twinkled. 'Should I rather ask which animal reminds you of me?'

'You're impossible!' She pretended to pout, though she enjoyed his teasing. It was a slight return to the easy manner which had once been between them, and realizing that they were both glad of the diversion she knew that they would be happy to keep it up a little while longer.

'All right, we'll agree to leave me out of the discussion,' Stewart grinned. 'Perhaps you'll tell me what you *do* mean.'

'Take the wildebeest – whenever I see it I feel like laughing. I had a boss like that once – a grumpy, bad-tempered man, who always looked as if he'd got out of bed the wrong way and forgotten to wash, and comb his hair.'

'Marvellous!' Stewart put his head back and laughed. 'You're quite right. The comparison had never struck me before.'

'Do you know what the vultures remind me of? Gossiping old women, who hover around the scene of a tragedy or a scandal, just waiting to sink in their claws ...'

'And then finish off their victims with their scandal. Right again.'

'And then the impala,' Emma went on, encouraged by his attentiveness. 'Do you know where they fit in?'

'No,' he said gently.

'They're like a corps de ballet.'

'They *are* beautiful, aren't they?'

'They're perfect, so very perfect. That one' – she pointed to an animal that was grazing a little way from the others, and was perhaps even more attractive – 'she's the prima ballerina, the special one.'

They sat a while in silence, enjoying the scene before them, and though the feeling of strangeness was still there in some measure, it was not as strong as it had been.

Presently Stewart said, 'Look, Emma.'

'Where?'

'There.' He pointed.

'I . . .' Her eyes swept the bush, but she saw nothing out of the ordinary.

'Can't you see it?' And when he saw her bewilderment, he said, 'The buck haven't spotted it either. There's a lion, Emma.'

'Yes!' she breathed, for she saw it now, moving slowly and stealthily forward, the tawny hair blending perfectly with its surroundings. 'Is it . . .?'

'It's preparing for a kill. And I think, I very much fear the victim will be your prima ballerina.'

'Oh, no! Stewart, no!'

'Yes. She's so apart from the others . . .'

He stopped abruptly. Things happened fast then. The herd becoming suddenly aware of the danger, the steely speed of the lion, the helpless confusion and plight of the lovely impala . . .

'Stop it!' shouted Emma, in the one moment before it happened, and when she thought the animal could still be saved. 'Stop it, Stewart!'

Desperately, when she understood that Stewart was going to sit by and do nothing, she tried to wrench open the door of the car. At the same moment Stewart's hand clasped hers in a vice-like grip that brought tears to her eyes, and when she looked again it was all over.

'Why didn't you save her?' she shouted furiously.

'You little fool!' he said angrily, and his face was white with fury. 'What the hell did you think you were doing? Opening your car door like that!'

'You obviously weren't going to do anything!' she

said fiercely.

'The lion has to eat.'

'But not *that* impala.'

'This is the jungle, Emma.' His eyes were like steel and his voice was taut. 'This is the jungle, with jungle laws. And the sooner you realize that the better!'

And then he had pulled her to him, and was kissing her, roughly, passionately, as if he would never stop.

Emma never knew how long the kiss lasted. When Stewart took his lips from hers she pulled herself up against her side of the car, numb, shocked, unable to think.

'Sorry about that,' he said, tight-lipped.

'The law of the jungle too?'

'I said I was sorry.'

'Take me back to camp,' she said flatly.

Without a word he put the car into gear and started back to Skukuza.

Miserably Emma stared out of the window. This was not love as she had pictured it, not the way she wanted it to be. So brutal, so ruthless. She had wanted Stewart to kiss her, she had been wanting it for so long now, but when his kiss came she wanted it to be tender, loving, passionate – nothing like the kiss she had just experienced.

The strangeness was back between them, and with it something more – hostility, tension, a sense of waiting.

Emma had never been so glad to see Skukuza loom in sight.

'Be seeing you,' Stewart said impersonally, as they got out of the car.

'Yes . . .' she said uncertainly. 'Thank you for lunch.'

He did not answer, but just strode briskly away from her.

When he had gone Emma turned and walked down to the river. Was it going to be unbearable to remain in the same camp as Stewart? Should she go home now, even though a few weeks of the three months still remained? Much as she wanted to, she knew she could not do it.

There were still photographs she wanted, animals she was hoping to see, pictures she was not quite satisfied with and wished to try once more. But the photographs, important as they were, were not the only factor involved.

There was something more, a personal obligation which she owed to herself. An obligation not to think of herself as a failure ever again. She valued her self-respect too much for that. Somehow she knew that if she left the Park now, she would always carry with her the feeling of failure, and the knowledge that she had allowed another person to influence her life.

Only a few more weeks. She would stay, and she would do her best to enjoy them. In spite of Stewart!

CHAPTER TEN

ONCE Emma had made her decision she found that she was, in fact, enjoying the little time that was left to her in the Park.

She did not drive around frantically any more, searching for animals, but would go to the places she knew, the hippo-pools, the water-holes, the slip-roads to the river. There she would sit for hours sometimes, watching the animals when they came to the water to drink, and enjoying the exotic birds who sang their wild and lovely songs as they perched on the branches of nearby trees. Most of all she enjoyed the sense of peace and tranquillity, and sheer timelessness.

She would miss this life, she knew that now. She thought of England and tried to imagine what it would be like to live there again. Hurrying along the streets of London, fighting to get on to a tube, huddling under an umbrella as she waited to cross a busy road. She would think then of the life she had tasted and grown to love, and would regret the basicness, the simplicity, the naturalness of it all.

Stewart. Stewart was an interlude, she tried to tell herself. She would have to forget him. She *would* forget him. At any rate, she would try.

Then there was Lance. She knew, with a twinge of conscience, that the memory of Lance would become ephemeral once she was back home. She had found herself spending more time with him since the days of the film and the party and the kiss by the river.

'Will you ever think of me when you're back in England?' he asked her once.

'Often,' she smiled. 'Whenever I think of my wonderful holiday here.'

'Emma—' he began, and when she saw the look in his eyes she knew a moment of trepidation and would have liked to stop him. 'Emma, do you think you could ever feel more than you do now? About me?'

'I'm very fond of you,' she said after a moment.

'Fond?' He looked at her quizzically.

'I like you, you know that.'

'You like me, yes. But . . . Emma, we both know what I mean. Do you think you would marry me if I asked you to?'

She was silent, not wanting to hurt him. If only things had worked out differently, if it was not Lance who had asked the question.

'Well, Emma?'

'No, Lance,' she said at last, as gently as she could. 'No. I like you so much as a friend, but marriage . . .'

'It's Stewart, isn't it?' he said quietly.

'I'm not marrying Stewart,' she parried the question.

'Then . . .'

'Perhaps I'm not ready for marriage right now. Lance, please, let's enjoy these last weeks together. We've been so happy until now.'

'Okay, sweetheart.' He looked quietly at her for a moment, then he smiled. 'We'll try to make these weeks happy ones.'

Dear Lance! Always so reasonable, so good-natured.

And then there was Johnny. She would miss the boy, with his freckled face and faded jeans, his funny smile and clever hands. 'I wish you didn't have to go back,' he said now, as they sat at the hippo-pool.

'Holidays come to an end. That's a trite saying, but it's true.'

'What is trite?' He leaned back, pencil in the air, look-

155

ing critically at the sketch in front of him.

'Well-worn. Nearly finished the picture, Johnny?'

'Just one more time here at the pool. The rest I can fill in later.'

'I'm going to miss it all,' Emma sighed. 'It's so beautiful, isn't it?'

'You don't *have* to go,' he insisted.

'Johnny . . .'

'You could marry Stewart.'

'I think we've had this conversation before. And the answer is still no. People don't just get married as a means to an end.'

'But if you really wanted to stay?'

'You'll understand when you're older.' Pity that things could not be as simple as they were in the mind of a twelve-year-old. 'Besides, Stewart wouldn't want to marry me anyway.'

'Sure he would. He . . .'

'Let's change the subject, dear. Where did all the rangers go this morning? I imagine I saw your dad leaving early.'

'Yes.' Johnny's brow puckered into a slight frown. 'They're after a wounded buffalo.'

'Oh!'

'I hope they catch it. Buffalo can be dangerous at the best of times, but when they're wounded . . .'

'Did quite a lot of rangers go?' she asked.

'Quite a few.'

'Your dad was one?'

'Yes.'

'And . . .' It was difficult to speak his name casually, but Johnny was not in a communicative mood, and she had to know. '. . . and Stewart?'

'He's there too.'

'Oh!' Would she always have this sinking feeling

156

whenever she knew he was in danger — although, of course, in a few weeks she would be ignorant of his movements. She wondered fleetingly whether he would write, whether she would have the heart to write to him if he did not respond to her letters.

'Oh,' she said again. 'Will they be all right?'

'I reckon they should be,' he assured her.

The morning wore on. It was a lazy, lovely day, not as hot as it sometimes was, with the enervating heat that sapped the strength of those not accustomed to it, and Emma was sorry when she glanced at her watch and realized it was lunch-time.

'Your twelve-year-old tummy is begging for its food, I suppose?' she teased him.

'Well, I am a little hungry,' he admitted. 'I haven't eaten for hours.'

'Not since breakfast,' she agreed smilingly. 'All right, Johnny, let's go, then. It's a pity in a way, it would have been nice to make a day of it.'

'I guess we could stay,' he began a little half-heartedly.

'No, Johnny. Not when you're starving. Next time we come I'll have to remember to bring some food with me.'

'Can we come again soon?' the boy asked her.

'The next time you're home from school.'

'Oh, good. There's not much time left before the competition closes.'

'We'll come again soon,' she promised.

'You won't go back to England before I've finished?'

'Oh, Johnny!' she laughed as they left the hippo-pool, and began to make their way to Skukuza. 'You're worse than an old woman when it comes to nagging! I've told you we'll come again soon.'

When they arrived at the camp they parted. Johnny

went his way, and Emma decided to have a light meal and lie down for a short rest in her room. In the afternoon she went out again for a short while, stopping her car near the river, and waiting for animals to come her way. She got back to camp shortly before the gates closed.

This was one of the times of the day she loved best – when the visitors returned to camp and crowded the shop to make their supper purchases, or sat on the spacious verandah, enjoying a drink and talking about their day. It was one of the times when the camp bustled with life, and Emma loved to walk around and watch the people.

She was wandering through the shop when she saw Lance. He was talking to someone, and she only waved a hand and smiled at him. He raised his head slightly and smiled back, but it was a strange smile, Emma thought, half-hearted and mechanical.

A few minutes later she saw other members of the camp personnel talking together, their faces strained and still. As she paused nearby them she caught the words 'accident' and 'injuries'.

'Has something happened?' She stopped abruptly, a premonition of disaster gripping her all at once. 'Forgive me, but I couldn't help overhearing your conversation.'

'There's been an accident.' One of the men turned to her, his face grave.

'Accident?' Her heart lurched, as if she already knew the worst.

'A party of men went out after a wounded buffalo this morning . . .'

'Yes! Yes, I know that!'

'One of the men has been hurt.'

'Badly?' she whispered.

'Pretty badly, from what we've heard. So far we've had no details.'

'Who . . .' She forced herself to say the words. 'Who

158

was it?'

'We don't know.'

'You don't know? But surely if you know about the accident . . .'

'Bush telegraph – you know what that means. We'll hear more by and by.'

They were obviously impatient to continue talking where they had left off before she had interrupted them, and there was nothing for Emma to do but walk on.

Instinctively, like a wounded animal seeking its lair before licking its wounds, she went down to the river, to the place by the fence which had become her refuge, and leaning her arms on the fence she stared unseeingly over the river and into the bush.

An accident. One of the rangers injured – badly injured. Fatally? And who? The question burned in her mind. Could it be Stewart? She had no way of knowing, no way of finding out.

She had no claim upon him by which she could go and demand, of whatsoever person of authority she could find, to be told the news as soon as it came. No claim. No claim of any nature. Except for one. The unofficial claim, the one that nobody could take from her. The claim of love. The fact that she loved this man above all else in the world, that some part of her would die if anything were to happen to him. The most important claim of all in a way, and yet one that could never be acknowledged, never be spoken of, never be stated.

Disconsolately she began to walk. Morning might bring more news, more concrete facts and details. Until then she could only wait, and pray. She knew too that whatever knowledge she might gain could only be gleaned by looking for it, by hovering about the shop, the office, any place where people might talk. For nobody would seek her out, nobody would look for her to tell her the news, bad or good as the case might be.

Emma slept little that night. Stewart's face was continually before her eyes – the strong tanned face with the smile that crept up at one corner of the mouth and made her heart turn over, the eyes that could be at times so arrogant and mocking, and at other times so unbelievably tender.

Would she forget him when she was back in England? *Could* she leave him if he was badly hurt? Possibly, probably even, Miranda would be at his side, nursing him, looking after him, seeing to his every need. But in spite of Miranda, in spite of his attitude to her, Emma, could she bear to be in England when he lay injured and broken beneath a different sky?

Emma thought the night would never end, but towards morning she drifted into sleep, and by the time she woke the sun was already high in the sky. The camp rang with the usual breakfast noises of the visitors, who were enjoying their holidays unaware of the disaster which had occurred, and while Emma had a hurried meal two blue birds chirruped and argued nearby, as they waited for her scraps. Realizing she was not hungry, she threw the remains of her breakfast to the birds, and hurried in the direction of the administration buildings.

'Careful!' She was in such a hurry that she did not look where she was walking, and before she knew it had collided with a person striding in the opposite direction. 'Careful, Emma!' A hand went out to steady her when she would have fallen, and momentarily an arm slipped around her waist.

'Stewart!' Shocked, she looked up at him, mindless in that moment of the emotions that flitted transparently across her face. 'Stewart! Oh, Stewart!'

'Yes, it's me.' He was smiling. 'You look as if you'd seen a ghost.'

'I . . . Are you all right, Stewart?'

'I'm fine. What's wrong, Emma?'

'I thought . . . I imagined . . . I heard there'd been an accident,' she faltered.

'There *has* been an accident.' His face was tired and grim. 'A nasty accident.'

She looked at him wordlessly, still too relieved by his presence to ask anything further.

'I see you've heard about it,' he said.

'Yes, last night. And I thought . . . I thought . . .'

'What did you think?' And as she looked at him tremulously a softness, the tenderness she had glimpsed only a few times before crept into his eyes. 'Did you think . . . Emma, did you think it was me?'

She could not answer, the emotion still so strong that she knew she would cry if she tried to speak. Stewart put his arm around her shoulder and said, 'No, Emma, it wasn't me.' He was silent a moment or two, then he said quietly, 'It was Mike.'

'Mike?' She looked at him uncomprehendingly for a second, and then, as the name took on meaning, she whispered, 'Oh, no, not Mike! Not Johnny's father!'

'Yes.' He had taken his arm from her shoulder and was lighting a cigarette, and she saw that the hand that held the flame was not quite steady. 'The buffalo had been wounded. When we got close to it . . . it charged. Mike tripped. It was an accident. He tripped over a twisted root in high grass. It's . . . it's one of those things that happen sometimes.'

'Is Mike . . .? Will he . . .?'

'He's alive. He's in hospital. He's in a bad way, but we're hoping he'll make it.'

'Oh!' Emma groaned.

'They're going to operate today,' he went on.

'Does his wife know? Does Jane know?' And when

Stewart nodded, she said, 'And Johnny?'

'Yes.'

The manner in which he said the word made her hold her breath a moment. 'Did Johnny take it badly?'

'I'm afraid so. He . . . he's very cut up.'

'He loves his father so much.' She was silent as she thought of Mike, Johnny's father, a cheerful man, a little older than Stewart, who was always ready with a smile and a friendly word for the girl who had befriended his son.

'What will they do – Johnny and his mother?' she asked.

'I'm not quite sure,' said Stewart.

'Will they stay here?'

'I shouldn't think so. Last night Jane was talking of going to stay with her parents till Mike recovers.' If Mike recovers. She knew the words were imprinted on both their minds.

'I must see Johnny.' She turned to Stewart suddenly, and tears stood in her eyes. 'Such a dreadful thing! I . . . I only hope Mike gets better.'

'That's something we're all hoping.' He lifted his hand and glanced briefly at his watch. 'I must go now, Emma. I just came to camp for an hour or so – things that needed doing – I must get back.'

'But . . . I thought Mike was in hospital.'

'He is. But the buffalo is still at large. In the confusion, after the accident, it got away. That shouldn't have happened either, but it did.'

'You're going after it?'

'We're pretty close to it. The trackers know where it is, but in the dark we couldn't take chances.' He reached out and drew her to him for a moment. Then he said, 'Be seeing you, Emma.'

She watched him go, her heart heavy with apprehension. He was almost out of hearing when she called impulsively, 'Stewart!'

'Yes?' He turned and looked back at her questioningly.

'Take care of yourself.'

He stood looking at her a moment longer, and the rare smile that she loved spread slowly over his face till it reached his eyes. 'I'll do that.' He raised a hand, and then walked away.

Only when Stewart was gone did Emma become aware once more of her surroundings. It was then that she saw Lance. He stood not far from her, looking as if he had just arrived on the scene. But on his face was a strange expression, and suddenly Emma wondered how long he had been there.

'Lance,' she said uncertainly.

'Hello, Emma.' He made no move towards her.

'You were listening?'

'I heard every word.' It was obvious from the way he said it what he meant. 'Very touching!'

'Touching?' she queried.

'Don't you think so?'

'I'm not sure I understand you,' she said, wondering, as she looked at the expression in his eyes, whether she had ever really understood him. 'A man has been badly hurt. I don't see anything touching about that.'

'Ah, but that man is not Stewart.' Still the expression lurked in his eyes. 'And that is all that matters, isn't it?'

'I'm really not in the mood for this kind of talk right now.' She pushed past him. 'I must find Johnny.'

'Jane!' Emma put out her hand to the other woman as she came into the room. 'I only just heard.'

'Emma, thank you for coming. I needed someone to talk to.' Jane's face, normally so pretty and cheerful, was distraught and white, her eyes red-rimmed and with shadows beneath them.

'You're packing?' asked Emma.

'Yes. We're leaving here as soon as my parents come.'

'Have you heard . . .?'

'Nothing yet. It's this waiting . . . this dreadful waiting that's so hard to bear.'

'I can imagine,' said Emma softly.

'All I want is to get to Mike,' Jane went on.

'Can I help you with anything, Jane?'

'No . . . Yes . . . You see, Johnny . . .'

'Where *is* Johnny?' asked Emma.

'I don't know.'

'You don't know?' Emma stared uncomprehendingly at the other woman. 'You mean you don't know where Johnny is?'

'I haven't seen him for hours.'

'I don't understand . . .'

'He was terribly shocked when we heard. The news came late last night. Johnny woke and heard . . .'

'Yes . . . I can believe he was shocked.'

'He's so close to Mike. He cried, Emma. He tried to be quiet. I suppose he was ashamed, heaven only knows why, and he didn't want me to hear him. As though I wouldn't know it was the normal thing for a boy to do! Anyway, I'm his mother. I knew.'

'But where is he now?' Emma cut Jane short.

'I don't know.'

'He must be somewhere in the camp, surely?'

'I presume so.' Jane looked about her vaguely. 'I thought perhaps he was with you.'

'I haven't seen him since yesterday afternoon – since we came back from the hippo-pool.'

'He must be hiding somewhere.' Jane was pacing about the room. 'He's a sensitive child. And he adores Mike. I imagine he's gone somewhere to be alone.'

'But we must find him.' Emma was more perturbed than she liked to show this woman who already had so much to worry about.

'He'll come in just now. Johnny's unpredictable. You never know when he'll walk in.'

'Of course,' Emma said reassuringly, sensing Jane's need to convince herself. 'I'll look around a little in the meantime. No harm in that. Perhaps he's hungry. If he is I'll see that he has a bite.'

'Thank you.' Jane tried to smile. 'Emma . . .'

'I'll send him along to you when I find him,' Emma promised.

'Thank you, I'd appreciate that.'

'But first, what about you?' Emma said gently. 'I'm sure you've had nothing to eat all morning.'

'I'm not hungry.'

'You must have something to eat,' Emma insisted. 'You must keep up your strength.' Without waiting for a reply Emma found a cup and a tin of coffee, and taking the cup to an urn filled it with boiling water. By the time she was ready to look for Johnny she had seen Jane drink her coffee and eat a sandwich. 'I'll look for Johnny now,' she said.

'Thank you.' Jane was grateful. 'Johnny always talks so much about you, Emma.'

'And I'm so fond of him.' She reached out a hand impulsively and touched Jane's arm. 'I'm sure he's all right. He's a sensible child.'

'Yes.' The anxiety in Jane's eyes belied her conviction.

'I'll go and find him now. And Jane, I know these are just words . . . but try not to worry. About Mike, I mean.'

'That's not so easy,' Jane said unsteadily.

'I know.' Emma had a vision of how she would feel if Stewart were lying in hospital, critically ill. 'Try and rest a little, Jane. I'll be back soon.'

Had she even then, when she left Jane, Emma wondered, looking back, had a premonition that she would not find Johnny? First she walked to the administration buildings, to the shop and the office, to the library and restaurant, any place where she thought that she might find him. She asked the men and women who worked at the camp if they had seen him. They all knew the boy, and would have known if he had passed their way. But nobody could remember having seen him.

By this time word had got around about the accident. Wherever she went she found it was the topic of conversation. Johnny was popular and people were sorry for him. If they had seen him they would have known.

Emma walked the length and breadth of the camp, past the many bungalows, stopping to ask visitors whether they had seen the boy. Here it was more difficult, for the holidaymakers did not know him, and she had to rely on a description. And there were many boys with freckled faces and faded shorts.

She walked to the river and paced the fence, searching the ground just beyond it, knowing as she did so that he would not be so silly as to hide there. But by this time she was getting a little desperate.

As the hours went by and nobody had seen the boy Emma became more and more alarmed. Eventually there was talk of sending out a search party if he was not found soon.

'I can't understand it,' she said to Lance, when she saw him.

'He's obviously hiding somewhere,' said Lance.

'But where? I'm getting so worried.'

'He's probably playing for attention, Emma. He'll

come when he's hungry.'

'Johnny's not like that,' she said angrily, wondering that she had never before realized how callous Lance could be.

The sun was high in the sky. All about the camp holidaymakers were busying themselves with the mid-day meal, and still Johnny had not been found. Emma grew more and more anxious. Jane, Johnny's mother, was beside herself with worry. Members of the camp staff were now searching all over the camp, but as yet no headway had been made.

The idea came to Emma all at once. Glancing at her watch, she saw she could just do it. Without pausing for something to eat she made for her car, only stopping at the shop to tell Lance where she was going. 'He may be at the hippo-pool,' she told him. 'I'm going there now to look for him.'

'How on earth would he have got there?'

'He could have begged a lift with somebody.' And as Lance looked at her doubtfully, she went on quickly, 'It's a chance. If he's not there I'll return right away ... Lance, if anyone looks for me ... if Stewart should come back and ask ... please, won't you say that I've gone to the hippo-pool and will be back late this afternoon?'

Was she going on a wild goose-chase? she wondered as she drove as fast as the speed limit allowed. Johnny had said he needed one more visit to the pool to complete his picture. He was so set on entering the competition. It seemed to mean so much to him. And now that he and his mother were going to leave the camp he might not have another chance to go on with it.

Was she endowing him with a certain heartlessness? Was she wrong in imagining that the picture would be on his mind when his father lay in hospital, critically ill? Other people might think it heartless of him, but they would not understand, for they did not know the child as she had come to know him.

Johnny adored his father – this she knew. The fact of his accident must have come as a terrible shock to him. And Johnny was sensitive. He might need something to help him get over the shock. His art meant so much to him. Was it possible that if he finished the picture his heart was so set on, this could perhaps give to him a sense of security to help tide him over the difficult time which lay ahead?

With this reasoning, it was not impossible that the boy might have looked for somebody who was driving that way, and asked for a lift. And yet, Emma wondered, if he had wanted to go to the hippo-pool, why had he not come to her?

And then she thought she knew the answer to this question too, for perhaps Johnny had been shy, wondering if she would think him callous in the light of what had happened.

Presently Emma came to the little path that slipped away from the main road and down to the river. With a sinking heart she saw from afar that there were no other cars in the little clearing. Nevertheless, she knew, she had to drive down, park her car, and climb the rocky outcrop where visitors were allowed to be, in case Johnny had, in some moment of madness, prevailed upon somebody to leave him there to finish his picture, with the promise that he would be picked up again later.

A little nervously she got out of the car and walked to the rocks where she had sat so often with Johnny. Usually a guard stood near the parking area, a rifle slung across his shoulder for protection in the unlikely event of something happening, but today he was not there. Perhaps it was getting late, and he thought nobody would be coming that way any more . . .

It was therefore with a sense of apprehension that Emma walked over the rocks, calling Johnny's name, starting once when a squirrel jumped across her way. In the distance a hippo lifted its head above the water and took a long breath before submerging itself once more. Nothing else stirred.

When she was certain that she had not missed the child, and that he was not at the pool, she turned back, heaving a sigh of relief when she was in the car once more with the door closed. However safe one knew a place to be, she reflected, one would need nerves of steel to be able to wander fearlessly, without any protection, in the middle of a game park.

Emma put the car into reverse gear and began to back it out of the parking area, wondering as she did so why the procedure seemed so much more difficult than usual. The car was moving slowly, haltingly, almost as if something were holding it back. Perhaps there were stones or drifts of sand that she had not seen when she had driven down . . .

She drove in reverse all the way back up the little slip-road, and then, reaching the main road, turned in the direction of Skukuza. The sun was in her eyes now as she travelled, the harsh and disturbing glare of the setting sun. Anxiously she glanced at her watch, and was relieved to find that she would get back to Skukuza before the gate closed.

It came to her after a while that she had seen no cars for some time. Obviously most people travelling this road had turned back long before, but she was not worried. She knew the length of time she needed to complete the trip back, and though she must travel to the maximum of the speed limit, she realized that she would make it.

The only thing that worried her was the strange jerking movement of the car. What could it be? She would have to have it checked when she got back to camp.

All at once, with a final splutter, the engine cut out and the car was still. 'Oh, no!' she groaned, pressing down her foot on the accelerator as hard as it would go. 'This can't happen here. It just can't!'

But it had. Helplessly she looked around her, wishing she could get out of the car and look into the bonnet to see the cause of the stoppage, yet knowing she could not do it, for she had come some way since leaving the hippo-pool, and a lion could be lurking anywhere. In any event, she understood so little about the mechanics of a car that even if she did look into the bonnet, there was little she would find.

Almost without thinking she glanced at the dashboard. Then it struck her. She was out of petrol! Of all the idiotic things to happen to her. How could she have set out without checking her gauge? Well, now there was nothing for it but to sit and wait until she was picked up.

Though she was annoyed with herself she was not worried. It was late, and she realized there would be no passing cars which could stop and help her, but she had told Lance where she was going. Once she was missed, as she surely must be, Lance would send somebody to look for her.

As she sat and waited her thoughts were more of Johnny than of her own predicament. Where could the boy be? What had the shock of his father's accident led him to do? She had been so certain that she would find him at the hippo-pool, had been so glad when the idea came to her, sensing that the thought which had come to her so intuitively would be the right one. And yet he had not been there. It was incomprehensible to her what could have happened to him.

Her thoughts turned to Stewart as she wondered

whether the group of rangers and trackers had found the buffalo. If only the worry was over and she could know that all was well, she thought, glancing once more at her watch.

The African sun sets in a blaze of glory, but once it has dipped below the horizon it becomes dark very quickly. So absorbed had Emma been in her thoughts that she had not realized how dark it had become.

Suddenly she realized that the blackness was all about her, oppressive and frightening. A glimmer of light still remained, so that she could see shadows all around her, no more than black shapes in the fast-gathering gloom, and nervously she wondered whether this shape or that was a bush or a lion. And then even the little light that had remained was gone. It was quite dark – eerily, strangely, unnervingly dark.

Would anyone see her when – if – they came? The 'if' was beginning to creep into her thoughts, though she tried to push it from her, for it was obvious that somebody would be along as soon as she was missed and Lance said where she had gone.

Yet the fact remained – would the car be seen? There was a clump of bushes just ahead, and beyond that a turn in the road. With no street lights an approaching car could pass without spotting her.

Perhaps she should switch on her lights. She did so, and then, moments later, switched them off again, for she was uncertain how the animals would react. What would be the reaction of an elephant who chanced this way and saw the two great pools of light beaming unfamiliarly through the darkness? Would it walk away or would it charge?

She did not know – that was the trouble. She did not know what an elephant might do. There was so much about animals that she did not know. Stewart would know ...

Please, Stewart, please come. Come soon. So much that she did know and thus was frightened to try. And yet in a few weeks it would not matter whether she knew these things or not. In England, in London, in the busy streets, it would not matter if she was in a quandary whether to switch her lights on or to keep them off, for the possibility of an elephant blundering into her car would not exist.

Please, Stewart. Please come. Of course he would come. How could she doubt it? He would return from hunting the buffalo, from putting the wounded animal out of its misery and out of danger to others, and on his return to Skukuza he would go to speak to Jane. Jane would tell him of Johnny's disappearance and that Emma was out looking for him. And then he would come looking for her, and when she in turn could not be found, word would go round the camp. Lance would hear, and he would tell Stewart of the trip to the hippo-pool.

That was when they would come to find her. She could see it all so clearly. She could see him running to his jeep and driving up to the gates, closed and bolted now for the night. She could see him tell the man at the gate that this was an emergency, that a woman was missing, that he must go out to look for her. And the big gates would swing open to let the jeep through.

Any moment now he would come. All she had to do was sit and be patient. And wait.

It is burning hot beneath an African sun, but when night falls it grows cold quickly. Now, in the car, with nothing warm to hand, Emma began to feel chilly, and because she had had nothing to eat since early that morning, she was hungry. Straining her eyes, she peered into the blackness of the bush for any sight of approaching light. Turning down her window – just an inch, for who knew what lurked by the roadside ready to spring – she tried to listen. But if a car was approaching she could neither see it nor hear it.

The bush became alive with sound. The continuous, familiar chanting of the crickets sounded all at once louder and more primitive, throbbing and pulsating, as if it spoke of all the unknown that was around her. Sounds that could be heard in the safety of a camp, with the security of fences and fires all around, were quite different, Emma discovered, when one had to listen to them alone, in the unfenced darkness. She heard rustling and crackling, the barking of baboons and the maniacal laugh of a hyena. Once through the darkness came the long low roar of a lion, sending shivers down Emma's spine. The lion could be far away, she knew, the sound of its roar echoing through the stillness, or again, it could be very near.

All at once she became aware of something watching her. Quickly she turned her head. Two pinpricks of light shone in the darkness. For a moment she was confused. Then she realized the pinpricks of light were the eyes of an animal. But what? Oh, God, what?

Stewart! Lance! Where are you? Come! Please come. Maybe I'm being hysterical, but I don't know how much longer I can bear it.

Once she was aware of an animal, massive and frightening in the blackness, nosing its way around the car, nudging the unfamiliar object, before it wandered away. She thought then that the night would never pass – that there would never be an end to this nightmare of sitting, quite alone, in the blackness, with wild animals roaming all about, and with no possibility of getting out of the car and looking for help.

It was not possible to sleep. Even if she had not been frightened, and gradually she found she was becoming accustomed to the nameless sounds all around her, she was too cold and too hungry to be comfortable. Now and again she would find her eyes closing, would find she had dozed off for minutes at a time, but actual sleep never came.

The false dawn comes early. Long before sunrise the blackness began to lift into a kind of transparent greyness, so that she could make out the shape of the bushes and trees around her. Not far away a klipspringer shivered beneath a tree, looked at her for a long moment, and bounded away. As it became lighter and lighter she saw the marks of many hooves nearby, and realized that the sounds she had heard during the night had not been imaginary.

Once she thought she saw a flash of movement behind a clump of trees. It was not light enough to see distinctly, but soon the movement became clearer and nearer. She saw the legs first, tall and thin and strong, and then as the bodies came clear of the trees, she watched three giraffes, stately and slow, nibbling at the tops of the trees. They stopped when they saw the car, standing motionless, with only their tails, like small bristly brushes, flicking in the stillness. Then, of one accord, they advanced to the road, scampered across it, and were lost in the bush on the other side.

More and more animals began to move through the trees, across the road, and to the river. Now that the darkness had lifted and the promise of help – for cars passed this way during the day – was near, Emma began to enjoy herself.

She had never been out quite as early as this before, for the gates only opened a little later. Stewart had told her once that the animals went to drink long before sunrise, and she realized that she must be near a drinking spot, so much game was she now seeing.

Three kudu, regal and beautiful, passed before her car,

and a rare and lovely sable antelope. A herd of zebra and wildebeest grazed in the bush not far away, and once a snuffling in the grass heralded the approach of a warthog. It looked her way for a shy, hesitant moment, then ran across the road in its stumbling gait, and was gone.

If only she dared get out of the car and open the boot for her cameras! She was toying with the idea – after all, it would take her only a minute – when she saw the vultures in the trees. There they sat, hideous and dangerous scavengers – waiting. She shivered suddenly in the early morning coldness. Somewhere, very near, there had been a kill, for the vultures were waiting their turn at the carcass. From their position in the trees so near her, she knew the kill could not have been far away. Even now, predators of some kind were in the bush nearby.

The hunger within her had become a gnawing pain, and she was looking at her watch impatiently, when she heard it. The rumbling noise of a car. Holding her breath, she watched as the jeep drew alongside her.

'Emma!' With a quick leap he was out of his car and into hers, and had pulled her into his arms. 'Oh, Emma, Emma!'

'Stewart!' She found she was crying with relief, and also with wonder, for she had never thought to see him so overwrought and emotional. 'Oh, Stewart, you found me.'

He drew away and looked at her, and she held her breath a moment, thinking he was going to kiss her, and then, inexplicably, he was holding her by the arms and shaking her and saying, 'Oh, Emma, you little idiot!'

'Stewart?' She looked at him in bewilderment, not understanding the sudden change of mood.

'You went after Johnny, didn't you?'

'Yes. Is he all right? Is Johnny all right?' she asked urgently.

'Yes, Johnny's fine.'

'Where did you find him?'

'He'd gone to see his father.'

'No!' She stared at him, wondering why she had never thought of this possibility. 'I don't see how . . .'

'He hitched a lift. He told a man who was leaving camp that he wanted to see his father, and asked to go with him to Nelspruit.'

'But why didn't he tell his mother?'

'Evidently there wasn't time. The man was on the point of leaving, and Johnny thought he'd ring his mother from the hospital.'

'Oh!'

'But there was some trouble with the lines, and he couldn't get through. He phoned last night.'

'But, Stewart . . . They were going to Mike anyway. Jane was packing . . .'

'I think Johnny felt he couldn't wait. Don't judge him too harshly, my dear. He was so upset that I imagine he wasn't able to be rational.'

'Of course,' said Emma. 'Poor Jane, she must have been so relieved when he phoned.'

'I think she was on the point of collapse by then,' he said quietly.

'Poor Jane,' she said again, imagining what the other woman had been made to endure all day. 'Stewart, how is Mike?'

'I can't say "fine", because he isn't. But he'll live – they know that now. He was operated on yesterday, and he came through it well.'

'Oh, thank God!' sighed Emma.

'Yes,' Stewart said soberly. 'It's been a miracle. The way the buffalo caught him . . . it was bad, very bad. We've been terribly worried about him.'

'Will he be able to come back here?' she asked.

'In time. I hope so – Mike is a wonderful ranger. But it *will* take time.'

'And Jane? Does she still intend going to live with her parents?'

'Yes, while Mike is in hospital. Then she can be near him.'

'So Johnny won't be able to finish his picture,' Emma said sadly.

Stewart looked at her strangely for a moment before he answered, 'They'll be coming back for a few days. There are a few things Jane will still have to see to.'

'So I can still bring Johnny to the hippo-pool, then?'

'Yes, if you want to.'

'Oh, yes. He only needed to go once more – he said so.'

'Was that why you came here yesterday? Did you have some idea that he would be here?'

'Yes. Yes, that's what it was.' She was silent a moment, watching a duiker step daintily through the long grass. 'I never dreamed he'd gone to his father. Stupid of me, wasn't it? Stewart, what happened to the buffalo?'

'We caught up with it finally,' he told her.

'Was it very difficult?' She thought of the density of the bushveld, and tried to imagine breaking a way through it in search of an animal that could be just about anywhere.

'We're very fortunate in that our trackers are excellent. I've lived in the bush all my life, but they see signs that I would miss. We found the buffalo, Emma. We knew more or less where it was, of course. We did – what was necessary.' He was quiet a moment. When he continued it was with anger. 'The utter senselessness of it all! It makes me so wild, so terribly wild. It was another instance of poachers forgetting a snare. And look at the resulting tragedy. A man's life in jeopardy, and the life of a magnificent animal ended in its prime.'

While they were talking it had become even lighter, and now, looking at him, she could imagine a little of what he had been through. For she saw the lines of weariness and sadness beneath his eyes, and the grey and haggard look upon his face, and her heart went out to him. Her eyes dropped to his hands and she saw that they were torn and scratched, a jagged cut running up his right thumb.

'You've hurt yourself!' she exclaimed.

He looked down, as if he had just noticed the cut. 'That was nothing,' he said quietly.

'You've had a rough time.'

'It was rough, yes.' He looked at her, and she was astonished at the anger that flared again in his face. 'It was rough, Emma. And when I got back to camp and found you were gone, and nobody knew where you were – how do you think I felt then?'

She stared at him uncomprehendingly as he went on. 'You can be so foolish, Emma. I was beginning to say that when I found you, and then I got sidetracked, talking about Johnny.' He gripped her arms and shook her. 'Little idiot! Don't you ever think?'

'I don't know what you mean.' Her lips were trembling.

'Did it never occur to you to wonder what someone else might be feeling?' he demanded.

'But ...'

'How do you think I felt when I got back to camp and found you were gone? I asked around and nobody knew where you were. Nobody had seen you go. The gates were closed, and your room was empty, and your car was not where you usually park it. What was I to think?'

'I'd gone after Johnny,' she stammered, still bewildered by his anger. 'I thought he might have gone to the hippo-pool. The competition ... He was so keen to finish his picture. And if he was leaving here he wouldn't be able to ...' She trailed off miserably. 'I guess I was silly, but we couldn't find him anywhere, and then I thought of this. It was a kind of last resort. I was wrong, though, he wasn't here at all.'

'I hit on the hippo-pool somewhere in the middle of the night,' Stewart told her. 'After I'd been lying awake for hours trying to imagine where you could be.'

'You were so worried about me?' she said wonderingly.

'You're even more of a fool if you don't know that,' he said abruptly. 'Somewhere around midnight I remembered your trips with Johnny, and I twisted the gatekeeper's arm to open the gates early, as soon as it was light enough for me to see.'

'Oh, Stewart,' she said with a sob. 'So you really did come here because of me.'

'Well, of course. Why do you think I'm here? But, Emma, why did you go out so late yesterday? You must have known you wouldn't get back?'

'It wasn't that,' she said. 'I ran out of petrol.'

He stared at her for a long moment. 'Emma, my little idiot of an Emma,' he said despairingly, with a tenderness that made her heart skip a beat. 'Is there no end to your foolishness? How can you ever be ...' He stopped and did not finish the sentence. 'Why didn't you tell somebody? Why didn't you leave word where you were going?'

'But I did,' she said blankly. 'I told Lance.'

'Lance?'

'Yes, of course. If only you'd asked him.'

There was a long moment of silence. Overhead the vultures soared in the rapidly lightening sky, and from the riverside the three giraffes she had seen earlier stepped gracefully back over the road, returning from their morning drink, and vanished into the bush.

'I did ask him,' Stewart said presently.

'You did?' She gazed at him in utter bewilderment.

'Yes.'

'What did he say?'

'Nothing,' he said shortly.

'He didn't tell you where I'd gone?'

'He only asked me why I thought he would know your whereabouts.'

'But that's ... that's incredible!' Emma felt numbed, shocked. That Lance could have behaved like this was entirely beyond her conception of him. 'Did he know I was missing?'

'Of course. I told him.'

'Then ...' The full enormity of Lance's betrayal began to sink in. 'He must have realized something had happened to me. He knew. He knew I was out in the bush ... alone. It could have been anything ... anything ... couldn't it?' she appealed helplessly.

'It could,' he answered her gravely.

'He didn't know that I'd run out of petrol. I could have had an accident ... a lion or an elephant, or ... or something wrong with the car.'

Stewart let her talk. He sat quietly at her side, letting her talk, letting the havoc of her thoughts resolve themselves in words.

'I didn't know ... I never thought he was capable of something like this.. Stewart' – she turned to him – 'did you know?'

'I hadn't thought of it. But now that it's happened, I'm not all that surprised.'

'You never really liked him, did you?' she said slowly.

'No.'

'And he – he didn't like you either. He warned me to

keep away from you.'

'Really?'

'Yes – on that first day. Why didn't you like Lance, Stewart?'

He did not answer immediately. Presently he said, 'There was something about him I didn't trust, but I was never keen to talk about it. You liked him and you would have thought I was trying to turn you against him.'

'Not after this. Stewart, he didn't like you. Sometimes I thought he hated you.'

'I think he did,' Stewart agreed.

'Why?'

'Jealousy,' he said shortly.

It took a moment for the impact of what he was saying to sink in. 'Jealousy? Of me?' she said at last, slowly.

'Yes. But not in the beginning.'

'Was there somebody else?'

'Miranda.'

'You mean . . .?' She could not finish the sentence.

'Lance was in love with Miranda. She's very beautiful, you know.'

'Yes.' The face of the other woman swam momentarily before her eyes. 'She *is* very beautiful.'

'And Miranda . . . At the time Miranda didn't seem to want him.'

'She was in love with you, wasn't she?' Emma tried to speak casually, but to her own ears her voice sounded brittle and cracked.

'She thought she was.' He went on after a moment, giving Emma no chance to wonder what he meant. 'At that stage Lance already resented me. We'd had a few set-to's, when I'd picked him out about his work – things that were slapdash or wrong. Then, when Miranda seemed to reject him, I think he began to hate me.'

'Oh!'

'And in the middle of it all you arrived. You were so innocent and pretty and appealing, and . . .'

'He decided to use me for his own ends?'

'Not entirely. He wanted to make Miranda jealous, of course, but he came to like you. He really liked you. And then, of course . . .'

'Then?' she repeated tonelessly.

'He saw that – *I* liked you. That was when he made a special effort to win you.'

Emma was silent, remembering the odd feeling she had had sometimes when she'd been with Lance. Like pictures in a kaleidoscope they flashed before her eyes – the drive to Pretoriuskop when Johnny and Stewart had been discussing an outing, the scene at the film, when Stewart had found them together beneath the rug, walks to the personnel quarters, when he had known they would see Stewart . . . Things were becoming clearer.

'But I still don't understand why he left me out here all night when he realized I must be in trouble, she puzzled.

'I don't know, Emma. But I imagine in his twisted thinking it was a form of revenge. Apparently he felt you preferred me to him. Was he right, Emma?' he asked very gently.

She looked away, knowing she could answer only the truth, and at the same time sensing the futility of it all. 'Yes,' she said tonelessly.

He took her hand in his and stroked it.

'I'm going to take this up with Lance when we get back,' Emma said.

'He won't be there,' said Stewart. 'He was leaving the Park at sunrise.'

'Leaving?' She was astounded.

'With Miranda.'

'No!'

'You see . . .'

All at once she knew she had to have a breathing space before she heard any more. She realized also how very hungry she was. 'You don't happen to have something to eat, do you?' she asked.

For a moment Stewart looked startled. 'Of course,' he said. 'I'd forgotten. You've had nothing to eat since last night. You must be hungry.'

'Since yesterday morning, actually,' she corrected him, 'and I'm starving.'

'My poor little Emma!' He laughed softly as he thrust his hand into his pocket and brought out a slab of chocolate and an apple. 'Emergency rations – another rule to remember.' He smiled as he watched her tuck hungrily into the food. 'I'm going to take you back to camp just now, but first there are a few more things I must say to you. Can you last out?'

'With this I can.' Already she was feeling better, and eager to hear what he wanted to say.

'I told you Miranda imagined she was in love with me, but she wasn't really. I'd done something for her once, for her and her brother, some time ago. It was something she was very grateful for, and she mistook her gratitude for love.'

He was silent for a long while, and when he continued at last he was looking out of the window. 'At first I allowed her to visit me. Mistakenly perhaps, but I was lonely, and . . . I saw no harm in it. I'm very fond of Miranda. But then – circumstances changed, and I began to find her persistence embarrassing. I tried to explain why I couldn't . . . Anyway, on the night of Linda's party I ended it.'

'But I saw you kissing her.' She said the words impulsively, without thinking, and wished she could have swallowed the words as soon as she had uttered them.

'So Lance followed us there too.' He looked at her steadily, and Emma remembered the look of bitterness on Lance's face. At last she understood it. 'I had explained things to Miranda. That kiss was a farewell.'

'And now she's with Lance?'

'He'll be good to her. He's weak and vacillating, but he really does love her, and perhaps . . . perhaps it's what he needs to pull himself together. I rather think things will work out for them.'

'You said – circumstances had changed,' she began hesitantly. 'What did you mean?'

'Don't you know, Emma?' He looked at her steadily, and the look in his eyes made her breathe faster. 'Don't you know?'

'I . . .' She could not speak.

'Must I spell it out for you, my darling?' He drew her close, and his arms were strong and firm. 'I love you, Emma. I love you so very much.'

'Oh, Stewart!' Her eyes were wet as he pressed his lips to hers, firm and hard, passionate and yet infinitely tender.

'Have I been such a brute to you that I've made you hate me?' he whispered. 'Say you love me, Emma. Please say it.'

'I love you,' she said brokenly. 'I always have.'

'And I you, from the very beginning. When I saw you standing so innocently in the bush, taking your picture. I've loved you always.'

'You never told me,' she whispered.

'I know. For two reasons . . .'

'Reasons?'

'I wanted to be sure that you weren't turning to me on the rebound – after Jimmy.'

'Oh, no, Stewart, no!'

'You . . . you seemed so happy with Lance . . . and yet

on our trip together I thought ... I began to wonder then whether you were just lonely.'

'I've been over Jimmy for some time now,' she said quietly.

'And – Lance?'

'He was never more than a friend.'

'I had to be sure.' He held her very close. 'Emma. Emma, my darling, I want you to be my wife. But there are things a game ranger's wife must know. Elemental principles that must be followed, rules to be kept ...'

'You said there were two reasons,' she reminded him.

'This *is* the reason. I – I've been brutal to you, my darling, but I felt you must know what will be expected of you.'

'That time at the gate ...'

'Yes. And all the other times. You thought I was being cruel, and I *did* feel dreadful. But there are rules. Mary ... Mary died because she did something foolish. I couldn't see that happen again.' He held her for a while without speaking. 'There's so much for you to learn. It won't always be easy. Emma, am I being cruel? Should I rather send you back to England where you belong?'

'No.' She clung to him. 'I couldn't bear it.'

'My darling.' He stroked her hair gently. 'My beautiful, funny, hungry, lovely darling. I haven't even proposed to you properly. In my high-handed manner I've been taking things for granted. Will you marry me, Emma?'

They drew away from each other and looked for a long moment into each other's eyes. She saw the strength and the steadfastness, the tenderness and the passion and the kindness of the man she loved.

'Yes,' she said. 'Yes, my darling. Yes.'

And then he was kissing her, hungrily, tenderly, passionately, as if he would never stop. She knew then that whatever lay in the future, whether their life together would be easy or difficult, it would not matter. For she would be with Stewart, with this man she loved above all else in the world.

Her arms went up about his neck then, and she was kissing him back.

HARLEQUIN OMNIBUS

A Jumbo Read!!

Eleanor Farnes

The Red Cliffs (#975)
... Alison had no particular interest in the old Devonshire cottage she had inherited; her work was in London. But when the overbearing Neil Edgerton wanted to buy it, she was faced with a sudden decision.

The Flight of the Swan (#1280)
... It took six months for Philippa Northern to change her life—to shed her mid-Victorian upbringing, develop her hidden self and find the happiness in living she had never before known. Then a jealous woman threatened to destroy everything!

Sister of the Housemaster (#1335)
... Ingrid hadn't met her sister-in-law's famous brother Patrick and didn't want to. She thought he'd be just as disagreeable as Sylvia. When they did meet, she knew she was wrong, though at first she wouldn't admit it!

Mary Burchell

The Heart Cannot Forget (#1003)
... Deepdene Estate should rightfully be inherited by Antonia's cousin Giles, but for some mysterious reason, he had been cast out. While living there, Antonia slowly uncovers fragments of the mystery, but everything that she learns is directly linked with the woman Giles plans to marry!

Ward of Lucifer (#1165)
... It was a struggle from the start. Norma knew exactly what she wanted, but Justin used her to further his own interests. He found, almost too late, that her happiness meant more to him than his own.

A Home for Joy (#1330)
... After her father's death, Joy accepted the kind offer of a home with her aunt and uncle and cousins. Only later did she discover that the offer was not as kind as it had seemed: there were certain strings attached.

HARLEQUIN OMNIBUS

A Jumbo Read!

Susan Barrie

Marry a Stranger (#1034)
. . . If she lived to be a hundred, Stacey knew she'd never be more violently in love than she was at this moment. But 'Edouard had told her bluntly that he would never fall in love with her!

Rose in the Bud (#1168)
. . . One thing Cathleen learned in Venice: it was very important to be cautious about a man who was a stranger and inhabited a world unfamiliar to her. The more charm he possessed, the more wary she should be!

The Marriage Wheel (#1311)
. . . Admittedly the job was unusual—lady chauffeur to Humphrey Lestrode; and admittedly Humphrey was high-handed and arrogant. Nevertheless Frederica was enjoying her work at Farthing Hall. Then along came her mother and beautiful sister, Rosaleen, to upset everything.

Violet Winspear

Beloved Tyrant (#1032)
. . . Monterey was a beautiful place in which to recuperate. Lyn's job was interesting. Everything, in fact, would have been perfect, Lyn Gilmore thought, if it hadn't been for the hateful Rick Corderas. But he made her feel alive again!

Court of the Veils (#1267)
. . . In the lush plantation on the edge of the Sahara, Roslyn Brant tried very hard to remember her fiancé and her past. But the bitter, disillusioned Duane Hunter refused to believe that she was ever engaged to his cousin, Armand.

Palace of the Peacocks (#1318)
. . . Suddenly the island, this exotic place that so recently had given her sanctuary, seemed an unlucky place rather than a magical one. She must get away from the cold palace and its ghost—and especially from Ryk van Helden.